MW00582404

Dreams Become a Nightmare
by Megan Johnson

Published 2015 by The Light Network
Copyright © Megan Johnson

Printed in the United States

Interior layout by Christi Koehl

Edited by Keidi Keating

ISBN: 978-0-9966403-4-3

To: Grandma and Grandpa
Here is my sequel! I hope you
enjoy it. I love you.

Megan Johnson

Dreams Become a Nightmare

Book 2 of The Dreams Trilogy
The sequel to Dreams Become Reality

What Do You Think Your Dreams Really Mean?

By Megan Johnson

I would like to dedicate this book to my loving parents, Mike and Sue, who are supporting me as my writing career begins to grow.

Acknowledgments

Thank you to Your Book Angel for doing an excellent job editing my book and for being willing to publish my first and second novel. To Brandon Stevens, thank you for supporting my writing and listening to my ideas as I wrote the book. And a special thank you to my fans who have been anxiously waiting for this sequel.

Megan Johnson

Chapter 1

*M*y body is trembling. I can't control my movements. What's going on? I feel like I'm on a roller coaster. My eyes are shut, and all I see is darkness. I slowly try to open them, but they're heavy. I go to move but realize my body is trapped by something...a seatbelt? "Open your eyes, Linda," I say to myself. I try hard. I hear screams belonging to men, women, and children. Then I hear a loud noise, like that made by a vacuum. My body is still out of control.

My eyes start to open. It's a blurry vision, but I'm in an enclosed space with people who are all sitting down. There's something hanging from the ceiling. I hear a man's voice. "We lost control, going down, everyone hang on."

My eyes open. I awaken in a white room. My heart is beating at what seems like a thousand miles per hour, and I'm sweating uncontrollably. How could I dream right now? Why am I still in this plain white room? Why is this happening to me? "SOMEONE PLEASE HELP ME," I scream out.

I look around, spinning in circles. I see all the same things over and over again. I cry harder and harder. I fall to my knees and I look up. "Please God, help me."

I continue crying as I lie down in a cradle position. "Please, please..." I start to fade away. I hear a buzzing sound and close my eyes to concentrate.

"Linda," I hear a smooth soft voice. Luke!

My mind becomes fuzzier. I hear another soft voice. "Linda, it's time to wake up now. Please don't leave me. I can't do this without you. You're everything to me. I love you. Please wake up."

The voice starts to fade. My mind is fading further. And then there's darkness...

I breathe calmly as my eyes open slowly. I hear a beeping sound and see a bright light. "I think she's awake!" says a voice next to me; a voice I'm so happy to hear.

I open my eyes and turn my head to the left. I see beautiful blue eyes, wet with tears, and a huge white smile. It's my husband and the father of my child. I'm back to reality.

Tears fall from Luke's mesmerizing eyes. He grabs my hand and comes close to me. "I thought I'd lost you. I'm so glad you're ok. I don't know what I'd have done if—"

"Shhh." I interrupt him before he continues his statement. "I'm back, Luke, and I love you."

He puts his forehead on mine, "I love you so much, Linda." He kisses me softly on the lips. I never thought his kiss would feel so good. Luke presses the buzzer for the nurse to come in. As we wait for the nurse to arrive, we stare happily into each other's eyes.

"Michael, is my baby boy ok?"

"He's perfectly fine. I can't wait for you to hold him."

"Where is he? I want to see him now."

Just then the nurse comes in. "Mrs. Jackson, I'm so glad to see you awake and alert. How are you feeling?"

"I have a bit of a headache but I'm ok. Where's Michael? I want to see him."

She smiles softly. "I figured you'd want to see him. He's right here."

Another nurse carries in my baby boy. He's dressed in a light blue onesie and wrapped in a yellow baby blanket. She puts Michael into my arms carefully. "Born June 30th 7 pounds 5 ounces," the nurse says with a sweet voice.

I'm amazed at how beautiful he looks. "Michael Bradly, my sweet baby boy," I say as I kiss his forehead. He's quiet, not crying. He looks up at me with his blue eyes, and forms a small smile. Tears instantly well up in my eyes.

"Luke, he's got your eyes and your smile. He's beautiful."

Luke rubs Michael's head, "He's amazing. He's got a good mixture of the both of us. We did a good job." Luke and I smile.

I can't stop staring into Michael's eyes. He takes my breath away. As I hold my baby boy, the nurse checks all my vitals.

"Everything look ok?" asks Luke.

"Everything looks great. Normal heart beat and temperature is good. I need to take your blood pressure and respiration rate."

I gently place Michael into Luke's arms. The nurse proceeds

with the tests. "Wow, your blood pressure is good and so is your respiration rate."

"That's good, right? Does that mean I can leave now?"

"Not that fast." The doctor walks into the room with a smile. He knows I'm anxious to get out of here. "You lost a lot of blood because of the placental abruption during the C-section. You were in a coma for three days. It's best if you stay overnight. This way we can keep you in IVs and continue checking all your vital signs before we send you off."

I roll my eyes and sigh. "Ok, I do feel a little weak." Even though that's the case, I want to leave this hospital and go home to my family.

"You should try and get something to eat and drink some water. Then you need to sleep some more."

"I'll go and get some food from the cafeteria," Luke says with a smile.

"Nothing too big though," replies the doctor.

"I want to hold my boy until you come back with the food," I say. When Michael is in my arms, I feel relief. It's the happiest feeling in the world. I rub his head and kiss his forehead. His little hand wraps around my finger. Tears form again and I smile. "You're going to have such a good life. I promise to always take care of you."

Luke walks in with a tray; a turkey and cheese sandwich and water. My stomach growls at the sight of it. "Woah, I didn't realize how hungry I was."

"Enjoy it, but don't eat too fast," Luke says. "I called your parents and May. I told them you're awake but that you're going to eat and get some more sleep. They'll be here in the morning when the hospital releases you. I'm going to stay here with you tonight. Then tomorrow morning we can all leave and start our new life together."

I smile as I chew my sandwich, "Sounds amazing. I can't wait."

I feel tired after eating. I yawn and lay my head on the pillow. "Time to get some rest," says the doctor.

Luke kisses me on the forehead, "Sleep tight. I'll be right here when you wake up."

I smile. "I love you."

"I love you too."

I close my eyes with a warm and happy feeling. I picture my beautiful baby boy in my arms. I picture my wonderful husband. Then I remember the dream I had when I was in a coma. How is that possible? Can people dream while they're in a coma? Does this mean anything?

I begin to feel nervous. My heart speeds up as I fade into sleep.

Screaming, panicking, my body is shaking uncontrollably. I try to open my eyes, but they're heavy. I feel like I'm dropping down a big slope on a roller coaster. My stomach begins to feel nauseas. Something is dangling in front of me, maybe oxygen masks. I open my eyes and see many people in their seats, screaming and crying, holding onto each other. I look around and realize I'm in an airplane. "We're all going to die!" I hear a man in the back say.

My heart is pounding. I look out of the airplane window and see nothing but fast movement. We're going down at a fast rate. This is it; this is how I'm going to die. Screams become louder, shaking becomes more intense. And then I hear a loud CRASH…darkness. death…

I awake abruptly and sit up in the hospital bed. Luke awakes from the chair. "What is it? Are you ok?" he asks with dismay. I look at him with a blank look, no smile, no emotion. "A dream? Already?"

I nod my head in agreement. "I had one while I was in my coma, and I just dreamed about it again, but saw the end result. The dreams are short, without much description or detail. But something serious is going to happen. In the dream I die, along with many other people. It was an airplane crash."

Tears begin to fall, "Ok, Linda it'll be ok. We'll take care of this. Try not to worry about it right now. Your parents and May are on their way. The nurses are packing up all of Michael's belongings. It's time to go home."

I try to smile, but it's hard. Straight out of a coma and I'm already having dreams; bigger dreams than before, with many more lives at stake.

Just then the nurse comes in to check all my vitals for one last time before they release me. "Alright Linda, you're looking healthy! It's time for you to go home now."

"Oh, thank goodness," I say with a sigh of relief.

The nurse comes in with Michael. "I think it's time for you to breastfeed. Now that you're ok and the doc says your fine, it's time you try."

I immediately smile. "Oh gosh, I'm nervous."

The nurse smiles back at me, "Don't worry you'll do great. I'll help you."

She puts Michael in my arms and I open my gown over my left breast. "Ok, now move Michael's head slowly so his mouth is on your nipple."

"Ok," I say nervously. Michael instantly starts to feed. It's a sore feeling at first and I feel a lot of pressure. But it's also a sense of relief. I look over at Luke and smile with tears. This is such a beautiful thing.

"You're doing great! Like a natural," the nurse says.

I smile and look down at my boy, my world, my life. Soon after Michael is finished, I hold him to burp him; Mom, Dad, and May come storming into the room.

"Linda, oh my god, aren't you a sight for sore eyes! We're so happy to see you," says Mom with tears. I hand Michael to Luke. I give Mom a big hug, then Dad, and then May. Tears fall like waterfalls.

"I'm so happy to see you all. I love you all so much!" They all take turns holding Michael, while I change into my clothes. It's hard to get up. My entire body is sore and weak. Luke prepares a wheelchair for me so I can get out of the hospital. I hate feeling this weak, but I have to deal with it.

"Thanks for everything," I say to both my nurse and doctor.

"You're more than welcome, Linda. If you need anything please don't hesitate to call. Take it easy at home for a few weeks until you regain your strength," replies the doctor.

"Oh, I'll make sure of that," Luke chimes in with a grin.

We all head back to our house. I don't ever want to let go of Michael. He's the most precious thing in the world. When we get home, I lay Michael down in his new crib in his beautiful bright yellow nursery.

We all sit around the living room as I rest on the couch. "Well, we'll leave you all alone now. I'm so glad everyone is ok. When you're feeling up to it, I want to have a nice welcome home dinner at our place," says Mom with a grin.

"Sounds wonderful, Mom."

I give Dad a hug goodbye and he has a hard time letting go. "I'm so glad my baby girl is safe and healthy. I love you so much." I hear a soft sniffle coming from him. That's very unusual as he's not much of a crier. And of course that makes me cry.

"I love you too, Dad."

I give Mom another hug, and May. "I'm so glad my big sis is ok. I knew you were strong, but you've proven to me that you're stronger than I imagined. You're my hero."

"You're very strong too, May. You've been through a lot, so don't forget that. We're sisters for a reason; both strong women. I love you."

After all the hugs and kisses goodbye I sit on the couch, completely worn out. Luke sits next to me and wraps me in his arms. It feels so comforting, relaxing, and safe in his arms. He holds me and we both drift into sleep.

All I see is darkness. All I hear is a loud CRASH.

Chapter 2

I awake to the sound of Michael crying on the monitor. "Wow, I feel like I could sleep for days," I say to Luke

"Well it has been a long three days for you. I'll go and get Michael and bring him down so you can feed him." What a great feeling it is having a baby to wake up to every day. I look forward to seeing my baby boy, feeding him, and holding him in my arms.

Luke hands me Michael carefully as I open my shirt. Michael starts to feed right away. "That's such a beautiful sight, I can't get over it," Luke says with a smile.

"I know, isn't God and life amazing? I can't thank God enough for watching over him, you, and me during the coma. I'm very thankful and blessed."

"Me too, babe. I'll make us some breakfast."

When Michael is done feeding I carefully put his head over my shoulder and lightly tap his back. Then I look into his eyes, mesmerized by his beauty. It's amazing that his eyes are such a bright blue already. He smiles softly and grabs my finger. "You're such a wonderful gift, Michael." I kiss him on his forehead and gently touch his cute square nose. He already has some dark hair that accents his tan skin. He's a perfect mixture of us both. He has my high cheek bones and nose. This poor child will grow up to be super stubborn though. I laugh quietly and think about how both Luke and I are stubborn and protective.

Luke peeks his head in as he mixes the salad. "What's so funny in here?"

"Oh, just thinking about how stubborn Michael is going to be when he grows up; I mean look at his parents," I say with a laugh.

"Oh my, you're right! Well one thing is, at least he'll know how to treat a lady right."

"Yes, his daddy is an expert at that."

"He winks at me and blows me a kiss from across the room." I pick up Michael and carefully bounce him around as I walk into the kitchen. Then I get a flash of the loud CRASH! I stumble, shut my eyes, and quickly sit in the chair. "My head is pounding."

Luke grabs Michael and places him in a crib we have in the living room. He then kneels in front of me. "Are you ok? Do I need to call the doctor?"

I shake my head carefully with my eyes tightly closed. "No, no, I think I'm ok." I rub my head. "Woah, that was really weird. I've never experienced anything like that before."

"What happened?"

"Remember the dream I had in my coma, and then I had it again that same night?" Luke nods with a worried look on his face.

"Well, last night when I went to bed all I saw was darkness and heard the loud crash. In my dream that's when I die. At least I think I die. I don't see or hear anything after that crash. Just now as I was walking, I heard the loud crash in my head and it gave me a shocking feeling. Then I got an immediate headache."

"That doesn't sound good at all. I wonder what it means?"

"The closest thing that has ever happened like this is the fire dream about us. I woke up feeling hot like my skin was burning, but it went away quickly. This hit me out of nowhere and sent a shock through my body."

He rubs my back for comfort.

"I'd hoped that having the baby would cure me somehow. Wishful thinking, I guess." I sit there and contemplate everything while Luke puts the dressing on our salads. Then I have an idea.

"Wait a second! What if having the dream while I was under made my gift more intense and heightened the ability to see even bigger things?"

"That makes sense, but if it affects your health then we need to try and do something about it," Luke says with a concerned tone.

"What can we do about it? No doctor can help. The only thing I can think of would be some sort of witch doctor. But that's stuff you see in a movie, and I don't believe in that." *At least I don't think I believe in that kind of stuff.*

"Witch doctor, huh?" Luke says with his eyebrow raised.

"You don't actually believe in that voodoo magic stuff do you?"

"Well, I mean look at your gift. You can consider that magic. I think we should keep all our options open."

I raise my shoulders, "Yeah I guess you're right. I can't be contradictive."

"Let's just eat and relax and see what happens. If this intensifies to where it really starts to hurt you, then I think we need to take that step."

"Alright babe."

I take a bite of the warm, soft pancakes that melt in my mouth. "So, want to tell me exactly what happened in your dream?"

I nod as I chew. "It was so quick yet intense. I was sitting in my seat in the airplane. It took me a while to open my eyes. All I felt was shaking. I heard screams from everyone in the plane. I saw the oxygen masks hanging from the ceiling. I saw crying faces. Then after a few minutes, I heard the loud crash, and then darkness. So far that's all I've seen. I have no idea where the plane is heading, what airport it left from, why the plane was going down, or the date."

"Phew, that's a lot to handle."

"And if my dreams still predict the future, then this plane crash is going to happen and I'm the only one who can try and stop it and save hundreds of people's lives."

"You haven't even been home from the hospital for a whole day. You don't need this added stress. What you need is rest for a while."

"I know, but Luke, people's lives are at stake. I don't know when it's going to happen. I need to try and take action now before it's too late."

"Alright," he says as he picks up our plates and takes them to the sink. "So what's your first step?"

"Since I don't have much information, I'm going to have to dream it again. Focus on the starting point of the dream, where the plane is leaving from, and the date."

"Do you think it's going to be that easy?"

"I hope so, but I have a feeling it's not."

"What about contacting the FBI?"

"I'd rather wait on that. I don't even know who my new partner is going to be. I don't think they'll be bothering me for a while. They all knew what was going on." *I get a chill over my entire body thinking of Tom and what happened.*

"All I can say is your new partner better be 50 pounds overweight, ugly, and mentally stable," Luke says with a joking tone. I laugh out loud with the images of Tom haunting my mind.

We rest on the couch watching anything but the news. I don't want to be disturbed by any crimes that have gone on in the area, because I'd somehow think that I could have stopped them. Luke holds me while I hold our baby boy. We decide to watch Friends; we can't go wrong with that TV show, as it always puts a smile on our face.

I soak up this warm family moment. I try to enjoy it as much as I can, because I have a feeling that what will come my way in the future won't be one bit peaceful.

I lay Michael down in his crib for the night. I soak in a hot bath to relax my body and mind. It is time to focus on the dream and get back to work.

It feels so good to lie down in my nice, big, comfortable bed. Luke pulls our feather comforter over us and I lie on his chest. "I've missed this. It feels like ages since I've been in this bed and in your arms."

He holds me tight and kisses me on the forehead, "I'll be right here when you awake from your dream."

I smile as I close my eyes. I see lots of people, the plane, and the oxygen masks. I hear the screams and feel the jolting of the plane. *Concentrate, Linda.*

***

I open my eyes and I'm sitting in a seat. I look around and see many people in a calm state. We haven't taken off yet. But I still don't know what airport we're leaving from. Usually the pilot comes on and announces where we're headed and how long it will take to get there.

I try to patiently wait and act calm, even though I know how this is going to turn out in the end. My heart is pounding with fear and anxiety. The seatbelt light flashes and everyone begins to strap themselves in. A medium height man, average build with long shaggy blond hair walks down the aisle toward the flight attendant, his short beard seems to reflect in the lighting. What's he doing?

He's wearing a long black overcoat with a Kelly green shirt underneath, and what looks like black combat boots. As he walks by me a stench of stale smoke overwhelms my nostrils. His look is blank with malice. I get a sick feeling in my stomach. Something is about to happen. People start to look around at each other, confused.

"Sir, we're about to take off. Please sit down and put your seatbelt on." He continues to walk forward.

"Sir please."

I can only see the back of his shaggy hair from here. But I see him put his hand behind is back. Oh shit.

He pulls out a pocket knife and stabs the flight attendant in the stomach. Everyone screams for fear. She holds her stomach as she falls to the ground. The other flight attendants try to rush the man, but three other men dressed in similar outfits come up and stab them in the back before they make it.

Screams grow louder, people start to panic. "Nobody move."

Four dead flight attendants lie in a pool of blood, and women and children scream with fear. The plane begins to ascend into the air. My hands are sweating, my heart is pounding. I didn't see any of this in my other dreams.

The shaggy hair leader puts his hands over his ears and clenches. "Everybody shut the fuck up!" It instantly gets quiet. "I can slit all of your throats if you'd like, but that isn't part of the plan. Now be quiet!"

I look around and see fear on everyone's faces; tears falling from their eyes, and people holding each other. I sit there frozen with fear. The four men gather in front whispering about their next plan of action, I assume.

What about the pilot. He hasn't said anything. Is he in on this too? Questions burn through my head. I need answers before I wake up.

I look at the middle-aged man behind me. "Sir," I whisper. He nods his head. "What airport did we take off from?"

He looks at me with a questioning look, "We just left..." And SLAM!

The ringleader kicks down the door into the flight deck. I turn my head with panic. Two of the men remain standing in front of the crowd. I hear scuffling coming from inside the flight deck. A few minutes later the men throw the pilot and co-pilot out in the aisle, blood dripping from the sides of their mouths, blood soaking through their shirts.

Screams from the frightened passengers grow even louder. The leader stands in front of us all, grinning and holding his bloody knife up for all us to see, "I'm your pilot now," he says pointing the knife from him to us. "I hope you all enjoy this treacherous, death ending flight."

Tears begin to fall down everyone's faces, and their bodies are trembling.

The plane begins to rumble. People scream. The oxygen masks instantly fall. The plane feels like it's speeding up. I see the bodies on the ground, rolling around from the turbulence of the plane. Then I hear the ringleader's voice, "Well folks, it looks like it's time. We lost control, we're going down, hang on tight," he says as he ends his statement with an eerie laugh that echoes through the plane.

People scream louder. "We're all going to die!" a man says from the back. I shut my eyes and begin to cry.

Rumbling, trembling, fear, tears... so this is what it feels like when you know you're about to die. I grip onto my seat so tight that my hands lose their color; then there's a loud CRASH, followed by nothing but darkness.

I twitch as I wake up. I'm sweating profusely, and breathing heavily. Luke puts his hand on my back. "Did you find out any information?"

I hear Michael crying on the monitor. "Stay put, I'll go and get him."

Luke brings him in and I feed him while explaining the rest of my dream.

I wait a few seconds to catch my breath before I begin. "Yes, I got a little. The airplane crashes because of a terrorist attack."

"Seriously? This isn't another 9/11 is it?"

"Oh gosh, I don't know. I hope not. I mean, I don't know where the plane crashes. All I saw out of the window is sky. I think they just hijack the plane on a suicide mission."

"Why in the world would they want to do that? With a random flight? No one in particular on the flight?"

"I don't know," I say with frustration. "I didn't get that much information. I still don't know where the plane takes off from or when. This premonition is much harder to figure out than my others. It's going to take a lot more effort and energy. I have a hard time finding the energy to even make it through the day."

I cry as Luke brings me and Michael into his arms. "It'll be ok.

You're not alone in this. We'll get through this together."

"I don't know if I should contact the FBI yet?"

"Well I think it might be time. You have descriptions of the terrorists and you know it's a large plane because there were a few hundred people on there. Maybe they can start narrowing down which airport it'll take off from."

"Yeah, I guess you're right. It's a good thing everyone at the precinct already knows about what I can do. It'd be hard to explain myself again. I don't know if I'm up to making a trip down there though."

"No, you don't need to be leaving the house yet. The detectives can come here."

I nod in agreement. I walk Michael back to his crib and immediately fall back asleep.

***

Less than a few hours later Michael is crying again. I roll over and give Luke a quick kiss. "I'm going to check on Michael," I say as I get out of bed.

"I'll make us breakfast. While we eat we can discuss what you want to do about calling the station."

I walk into the yellow nursery. The sun is shining through the blinds, and lightens up the room even more. It instantly makes me smile. I look down at Luke with his eyes wide open. He isn't crying anymore, which is a surprise.

I pick my baby up and pull him close. I kiss him on the cheek and set him down to change his diaper.

Then I sit in the wooden rocking chair in the corner of the room and feed him. The aroma of sausage and pancakes wafting from the kitchen makes my stomach growl. I head down to the kitchen carrying Michael in my arms. I take one step down the stairs and then it hits me hard.

Screams, his laughter, CRASH... My head feels like it is going to explode. I stumble and lose my balance, which sends a shock down my body. And then I fall.

Chapter 3

My head is pounding. I slowly open my eyes regaining my vision. I instantly feel a pain in my back as I try to move. I feel a cool wash cloth over my head. "Shh, it's ok." Luke's voice relaxes me.

"What… what happe-" before I finish my sentence I remember what happened. I shoot up quickly when I realize that I fell with Michael in my arms. "Oh my God. Michael? Is he ok? I dropped my baby, what kind of mother am I?" Tears stream from my eyes.

"Linda, relax. Michael is fine. Even though you blacked out, your instincts took over. You fell back holding on tight to Michael. All your weight landed on your back and head. That's why you were knocked out instantly. Michael was nicely cushioned, but I can't say the same for you. Those stairs are hard even though they're carpeted."

I lie back down exhaling with relief. I grab my head again. "Oh, I feel such a sharp pain in my head."

"Maybe we should get you to a hospital and have them take a MRI scan for your head just in case there's a concussion?"

I shake my head. "No, I don't need to go. I'll be fine."

"Linda, you've been home for what, two days? If that. You just had a baby and got out of a three day coma. I'm taking you to the hospital to make sure everything is alright. I won't ever let you have another scare like before."

I roll my eyes knowing I won't win this conversation. "Alright, but what about Michael?"

"We can call your parents and have them come over and watch him. Your mom will take good care of him. We should only be a few hours at the hospital as long as everything is ok."

I cringe at the thought of letting Michael out of my sight. I carefully leave the couch grunting with the pain from my back and head, and I take Michael out of his crib in the living room. I hold him close and close my eyes. A small tear falls. I don't know what I'd have done if Michael had gotten hurt. I lay him down as my emotion switches to anger.

"All of this because of my stupid so-called gift. What's going on with me, Luke? Why am I having flashbacks? It's almost an electrifying feeling. My mind flashes with light then the image from the dream. Do you think there's something seriously wrong with me?"

"I don't know, Linda. I'll feel better after you have a MRI scan done."

"I guess I will too. I just don't understand, and I'm scared to death," I say with a sigh.

"I know you are babe, and I'm scared too, but I promise you we'll get to the bottom of it."

"Thank you," I say as I pick up the phone and call my Mom.

"Of course I'll watch Michael for a few hours," my Mom says with an exciting voice. Wesley and I are on our way over now."

I breastfeed Michael one last time before we leave for the hospital. "Don't worry, Michael will be in good hands," Mom says as I walk out the door.

"I know he will. Thanks Mom."

We walk into the ER at Medical University of South Carolina (MUSC). It's a good thing Luke has ties at this hospital and that I recently just left, because Doctor Hue calls me in right away. He has been with me during the whole pregnancy.

"Ok Linda, tell me exactly what happened and where you're hurting?" I give a quick questioning glare at Luke. *Do I tell the doctor that I blacked out and fell?* I think to myself. I don't know if I want to go through the trouble of explaining what has been happening and my dreams.

I take a large gulp before I speak. "I was walking down the stairs with Michael, and I guess I'm still a little weaker than I thought. I slipped and fell. I held Michael close and made sure I fell on my back so he'd be protected. When I hit my back, I banged the back of my head as well. I lost a little consciousness. My head is pounding, and my back is sore." I glance at Luke and he nods his head up and down accompanied with a small smile.

"Ok, well it's a good thing you came here. Let's get this MRI done to make sure everything is ok. You'll hear some loud noises but it's nothing to worry about. The MRI will take about thirty minutes. Please make sure you take off any jewelry or metal that you're wearing."

"Ok, thank you Doctor." He has such a calming tone to his voice. His bald head, smooth face, and relaxed smile is comforting to me.

I remove my wedding band and take out my diamond stud earrings handing them to Luke. He gives me a reassuring wink and smile.

As the machine comes over my head, I begin to feel slightly nervous. The loud sounds are annoying, but I can deal with it. It's better than getting flashes of my dreams. I try to close my eyes and relax until it is over.

"Now that wasn't so bad was it?" the radiologist tech asks as I sit up.

"Actually it's the most relaxed I've felt in a while. I know that's weird," I say with a small laugh.

He shakes his head and smiles. "That's not weird at all. I've heard that many times."

"That's good."

I head back in to see Doctor Hues. "How long will it take to get the results back?"

"Well, since you and your husband are special friends of mine I'll have the radiologist and neurosurgeon read them right away. You should hear from me by tomorrow morning."

"Great, thank you!"

"Anytime Linda, now go home and get some rest. Luke, don't let her sleep for more than thirty minutes at a time, just for tonight."

"Alright Doc, thank you."

I nod my head in agreement as Luke and I walk away. "I'm sick of hearing to get some rest. I want to be back to 100 percent."

"Why am I not surprised? You're so impatient," Luke says with a soft laugh.

"Hey now, you'd be anxious if the tables were turned," I say jokingly.

"Me? No way." We both laugh.

Then I put my hand on my head. "Ouch! I never thought laughing would hurt my head. It must have been a hard hit."

"Well that's why we're going to do nothing but relax."

"Is it bad that I've only been away from Michael for a few hours and I already miss him?"

"Not at all. I miss him too."

We walk into my house and my Mom and Dad are sitting at the kitchen table making meat sandwiches. Michael is fast asleep in his crib. He looks like an angel wrapped in his baby blue blanket.

"Thanks for watching him for us," I say.

"I'd love to watch him anytime! I'm already obsessed with him," my Mom says with a cheesy grin. "He loves playing with my dangly earrings."

I smile. "You and your bling!"

"Here, have a seat and eat some lunch with us? Turkey or chicken?" Dad asks.

"Chicken for me."

"Turkey for me, thank you."

"So Linda, how are you feeling?" Dad asks with concern.

"I'm very sore, but I have a good caretaker," I say as I put my hand over Luke's. "I'll get my results back tomorrow morning."

"Oh good, that's quick."

I take a few bites of my sandwich. I soon feel lightheaded and put my hand on my head. "I don't feel so good."

"Honey, you're as pale as a ghost. Wesley, can you help me take her to the couch?"

He gets up quickly without answering. They both carefully assist me to the couch. "I think this was a little too much too fast," Luke says with an upset tone.

"Babe, its ok. I just need to lie down for a bit. I'm going to close my eyes and rest."

"Ok, but I'm waking you up in thirty minutes, doctor's orders."

Darkness floods in before I can respond.

I'm sitting in a busy airport. The sounds of people talking and flight attendants calling out flight numbers ring in my ears. I look around and see some people rushing and shoving their way through the crowd to reach their flight on time. Others are walking calmly. Once I realize where I am I stand up quickly. This is my chance to find out where the flight takes off from!

As I search through my bag to find my ticket, I recognize a stale smoke stench that makes me gag. I look up cautiously as I see the shaggy haired, creepy ringleader walk by me. He takes a seat one row behind me. I feel his cold glare on my back. My hairs raise and a chill rushes through my body. I shake my head to get back on task. I find my boarding ticket. Delta airlines: destination Denver to Washington National (DCA). Flight number: DL1428. Date: July 5th, 5:00pm.

Shit, this is only a few days away. I hear the flight attendant call our flight and my mind begins to fade.

I wake up to Luke shaking me. "Ok it has been thirty minutes."

"That was all I needed."

Luke raises an eyebrow. "What?"

"I found out more information about that flight. I need to get a hold of someone down at the station. This is going to happen within the next three days."

His eyes grow large. "Oh shit." My parents walk in when they hear us talking.

"How are you feeling?" asks Dad.

"Better, but Luke and I have to take care of some business right away."

"Business? You mean the FBI? Already? Do you think you're up to this?" Dad says with concern.

"I don't have a choice. This isn't like any of the other cases. This is bigger and involves many more lives."

"Ok, just be careful. We're here if you need anything," Dad says as he gives me a soft hug. There's no greater feeling than my father's love and protection.

After they leave, I feed Michael quickly and give the station a call. "Charleston Police Department, this is Detective Fredrick speaking."

"Hi Detective Fredrick, this is Linda Br… I mean, Linda Jackson." I still can't get used to saying my new last name.

"You mean the previous Linda Brown? *The* Linda Brown?"

"Yes, that's me."

"Wow, we weren't expecting a phone call for a while. Your husband Luke contacted us while you were in the hospital. I'm glad to hear that you're ok. What can I do for you?"

"I have a very important dream to talk to you about. This is bigger than any other case I've done. We're going to need some help."

His tone becomes deeper. "Alright Linda, can you come down to the station?"

"I'm still pretty weak. Can you and your partner come to my house?"

"Sure thing, we're on our way."

"Well, they're on their way," I say.

Luke puts Michael down in his crib. "They?"

"My new partners, Detective Fredrick and Arnold."

"Oh I see, double trouble now," Luke says with a wink.

"Don't even go there."

"I'm just messing with you, babe."

I gather some chairs around the kitchen table as Luke puts on a pot of coffee. Before long there's a knock at the door. "Linda, it's Fredrick and Arnold."

I take a deep breath before I open the door. Luke is standing right behind me. I take a few seconds to clear my mind and realize that from this point on that my life is about to change direction again. I open to the door to two men dressed in black pants and black t-shirts. I see their badges attached to their hip. "Hello Linda, I'm Detective Fredrick and this is Detective Arnold." I shake their hands as they enter.

Fredrick is definitely the lead man of the two. He's about 6 feet tall with short dark hair. He has dark eyes and eyebrows and a vague smile. He's got the tough man look. I can tell he likes to workout. On the other hand Arnold has shaggier brown hair and a beard. He's medium height and a little overweight. He has a wide smile and a goofy personality. People say you can tell a lot about a person in thirty seconds of meeting them, and I think I'm going to like working with these two.

"It is very nice to meet you both. This is my husband Luke," I say as they shake hands. I show them into the kitchen. "Would you like some coffee?"

"Yes please," says Fredrick with a stern tone.

"That would be wonderful. I could get used to this. I think I'm going to like having you as a partner," says Arnold with a joking tone.

Fredrick gives him a glare of annoyance. I chuckle. "I can already tell I'm going to enjoy working with you two."

We all sit around the table. Fredrick takes a sip of his coffee, "First, I want to say thank you for being so brave and going against someone like Tom. I can't imagine how hard that was, and fighting him off like you did was very heroic."

Chills run down when I hear his name. "Thank you," I say uncomfortably.

"Ok, so tell me what you saw in your dream. Was it a murder?"

"Oh, it's way beyond that." I begin to explain the first dream and how I experienced the crash first. Then I explain about the men, which airport, and when it's going to happen. They both sit there drinking their coffee and listening intently.

"Wow, I wasn't expecting that. That's only three days away," says Arnold.

"Do you think you'll be able to stop it in time?" Luke asks.

"We sure as hell are going to try. I believe we can. The only issue is we're going to have to contact the Denver Police Department. I don't know how they're going to handle something that hasn't even happened yet. It's going to look strange that they're getting a call from a Detective all the way across the country."

"Oh yeah, I didn't think about that. You 're the only people who know about my gift. Could this possibly get out to the nation?" *Would I be known nationwide? Would I want that kind of press and attention? That would make my life much more stressful.* Tons of thoughts and questions run through my head.

"Honestly, there's a possibility. They're going to know why and how we know about an attack in their area," Fredrick says with concern.

"Can't you tell a lie? I mean, do you have to give them my name?"

"I don't know. I'm going to need to think about this."

"Dude, there isn't time to think," says Arnold.

"You don't think I know that?" Fredrick says with a sigh.

"If Linda's name gets on national news, the phone calls won't stop, and neither will the press, which could open up an even bigger target for Linda. I mean, think about Tom. I'm sure there are more crazed killers out there," Luke says with frustration. "Linda doesn't need all that right now. This is awful timing. She could have just forgotten about it and got some rest like the doctor asked, but she cares too much about other people. She's helping you and the country out tremendously. I'm sure you can find a way to protect her."

Fredrick nods his head in agreement. "You're right, Luke. I can figure out something." We take a while to brainstorm what to say to the Denver Police Department.

Michael starts to cry and I pick up him and bounce him around. Luke leaves the two detectives alone to discuss the situation and comes to me. "Thanks for what you said back there. Everything you said was true; I don't know how I could deal with that. It'd put a burden on all of us."

"No need to thank me. I had to say my peace." I kiss him and then he touches Michael on the head and kisses his forehead. "Look at our miracle. I'd never put him or you in harm's way."

"I know you wouldn't," I say with a smile.

Fredrick walks into the living room, "Sorry to interrupt but we've come up with an idea."

We all walk into the kitchen and take a seat. "Alright, let's hear it," I say letting out a deep breath.

"We're going to fly over there and talk to them in person. We're going to bring the case to them instead of over the phone. I think that will help. I'm going to type up all the details you gave me, including the description of the men. I'm going to explain that we've had a lead on these men and have been following them; and that we believe they're going to attack this plane next."

"And you think that will be good enough?"

"No, I know they're going to bombard me with questions, but Arnold and I are both good at bullshitting."

"Hells yeah, we are!" Arnold says with a high-pitched voice.

Fredrick rolls his eyes, and I smile. "Anyway, we're going to make it work, I promise you."

"Alright, promise me you'll call and keep me updated."

"I will. We're going to take the first flight out of here tomorrow morning. That gives us two full days to convince them to stop these men."

"Good luck and thank you for keeping my name out of it."

"Thanks and of course." They both walk out of the door.

"So the waiting game begins," I say to Luke.

We order pizza, and night falls quickly. Luke has the alarm set to go off every thirty minutes. "I think I'm ok, as my head isn't hurting as bad as this morning."

"I don't care, I'm not risking it," says Luke. "Hopefully we'll hear from the doctor first thing in the morning."

***

After a long night of waking up, going back to bed, and feeding Michael I feel more restless than ever. I glance at the clock and it reads 7:00am. My phone rings. "It's the hospital," I say with relief.

"Hello?"

"Good morning, Linda. I hope I didn't wake you."

"I was already awake. I'm anxious to hear the results."

"Well, I have some good news. There was no bleeding in the brain, and just a minor concussion. You're very lucky."

Instant relief overtook my body. "Oh, thank goodness. So I don't have to worry about waking up every thirty minutes?"

"Nope, you're clear to sleep! Just remember to take it easy."

"Will do Doc, and thank you." I hang up the phone and then tell Luke the news. "I'm all clear! Just a minor concussion."

"Thank God, I'm so glad to hear that." I hear Michael crying on the monitor. "I'll get him," Luke says.

This day consists of nothing but lying in bed, watching TV, and eating. I haven't heard anything from my partners but I figured I wouldn't until tomorrow anyway.

My eyes become heavy and I begin to fall asleep.

Shaking, rumbling, screams, fear. I look around in panic when I don't recognize any of these people. I see the oxygen masks hanging. I see dead flight attendants on the floor. The same men are standing in front of us. But I don't recognize any of the same people. Is this a different plane? Did they make a switch at the last minute? One of the men throws the pilot and co-pilot out into the aisle. What plane am I on now? I begin to breathe heavily and start to sweat.

I feel an immediate drop of the plane. My stomach turns to knots as I embrace myself for what's next. We're going down fast, faster than I remember. I feel like I'm on a never ending drop on a rollercoaster. My breathing becomes frantic, my heart is pounding. I scream out loud. CRASH!

Chapter 4

My body twitches uncontrollably as I wake up. "Shit, this isn't good," I say out loud.

Luke looks at me with a worried expression. "What is it?"

"I just had another dream about the plane, except this was a new plane. They must have made a switch at the last minute."

"I wonder why they switched. Something must have triggered that."

"I need to contact Fredrick, but the only problem is I don't know what plane, or if it was even at the same airport."

"You still need to call them and let them know. We don't want them telling the Denver Police Department the wrong information."

I nod my head and sigh. "You're right." I pick up the phone and call Fredrick.

"Hey Linda, is everything ok? It's seven in the morning," he says with a yawn.

"I had another dream."

As I explain, Luke brings in Michael. Breastfeeding is starting to become second nature to me now.

"Shit, this isn't good. We've already talked to the police here in Denver. We're all planning on going to the airport tomorrow a few hours before that flight departs."

"Well it has to be that same airport. The structure of the inside of the plane seemed the same."

"Linda, many planes look the same on the inside, it doesn't matter what airport they're at."

"Oh."

"Let's hope luck is on our side tomorrow and they choose a different flight here in Denver. The good thing is everyone now knows what the men look like. It should be easy to spot if they're there."

"Ok, I'll try and dream the situation again tonight and if I find out anything I'll call you right away."

"Ok try hard," Fredrick says with a cold tone.

I look at the phone and sigh. "Well alright then," I say.

"What is it?" asks Luke.

"He seemed rude."

"I'm sure you misunderstood. He's probably frustrated because he wants to catch these men before a tragedy happens."

"And you think I don't? It's not my fault that I dream what I dream. I try to control it, but sometimes it doesn't work out perfectly."

"I didn't say that, Linda."

I get out of bed and walk around with Michael. "I know, I'm sorry. I can't stand this. Will it get any easier?"

"I don't know sweetie," Luke says as we walks towards me. "But what I do know is that we have a wonderful family who supports you."

I smile. "And that's all I need," I say as I kiss him.

As we all watch TV May walks in the house with Charlie. She's all smiles and an aura of happiness flows into the room. I'm so glad to see May happy. She deserves it after everything she has been through. Images of May tied to that chair in the hole, beaten, bruised, and malnourished make my stomach queasy. I'm glad that's over with. "Hey sis, hey Luke. Hiiii Michael," May says with a high pitched tone.

"Hey, what are you all doing here?"

"I just wanted to check in on you and see how you were doing."

She gives me a kiss on the cheek. "Thanks May, I'm doing fine. I've been taken good care of." Charlie stands behind May. He's tall and blonde, with blue eyes, and tanned skin; the magazine image of a surfer boy. He even talks like one, but he's a good guy. "Hey Charlie, how have you been?"

"Good. Ya know just keeping your little sis in line," he says with a wink.

I laugh. "Good! She needs it."

May rolls her eyes, "Yeah, yeah it goes both ways, stud." We enjoy each other's company for a while longer and get Chinese food to take out.

After they leave I look at Luke. "Well, it's now time to get focused and concentrate on this dream. If I don't find out something tonight, hundreds of people might die."

"I'm sure you'll find something out. When you're determined, it usually happens."

"I hope you're right." I feed Michael one last time for the day and lay him down in his crib.

Luke rubs my back to help me relax. My eyes become heavy and visions of the plane start rolling through my mind.

I can smell the salt in the air from the ocean. I feel the warm sun on my face, and a soft warm breeze. I open my eyes and all I see is blue. I panic and get up quickly. I look down and notice I'm wearing a bathing suit. I look all around this big open ship. There are hundreds of people, drinking, laughing, having a good time. A cruise? I see two big pools in the middle of the boat, with a spiral slide ending into the pool. I hear children laughing, a Caribbean band playing vibrant music. Why am I here? There has to be a reason, and usually it's not a good reason. I start to look around for signs. I glance up at the sun and shut my eyes for a second.

I hear Michael crying on the monitor. I wake up and quietly move out of the bed. Luke is still fast asleep. I sit in the rocking chair and feed Michael. "How's my boy doing? Thank you for waking me because I don't need to be dreaming about fun vacations on a cruise, I need to help save some people." Even though he has no idea what I'm saying, I feel a special connection to him. I know every mom says that about their child, but there seems to be something more between us.

When he's finished he looks into my eyes. We look at each other for what seems like twenty minutes. I kiss him on the forehead and lay him down.

My eyes become heavy instantly.

"Please fasten your seatbelts, we're about to take off." I open my eyes to see the flight attendant speaking through the microphone. I look around the plane and notice a long shaggy, blonde-haired man sitting very close to the back. It's dark outside, which means it's either very early in the morning or a late flight. I pull out my ticket stub just as the man is walking up front. Oh shit, hurry Linda before this all happens again. Six am flight, July 5th, Delta. All of a sudden my eyes blur as I read the ticket. I feel a small nudge, as if someone is tapping me on my shoulder. I shake my head to try and refocus, but

all I see is black.

I wake up and immediately open my eyes. I look over to see if Luke is awake, but he's fast asleep. *Someone nudged me to wake me up. How in the world did that happen?* I look at my clock. It's 4:30am. I've got to call Fredrick now! As I dial the number, I realize that I woke up just in time. Who knows how long I'd have had that dream for? It's strange that I woke up without any outside interruptions or before the dream ended.

I hear a yawn. "Please tell me you've got something," Fredrick says with a tired, stern tone.

"Yes, but you've got to hurry. They changed their flight time to a six am flight, and all I know is that it's Delta. I didn't get a flight number."

"Fuck, we have to hurry. Thanks Linda, we'll be in touch."

"Good luck." He hangs up without saying anything else.

Luke starts to move around when he hears the talking. "Everything ok?"

"I just gave Fredrick as much information as I could. Now we'll have to wait and see if they can stop them. I've done as best as I can."

"Yes, so you have no need to worry. It's still early, so try and go back to bed." I nod and put my head back down on my pillow with a strange feeling in my head. *What's going on with my dreams? Everything seems so different. I'm getting bigger cases, and now something is waking me up so I send on the information before it's too late. An angel? A ghost? Something is different and I'm determined to figure out what it is.*

***

A few hours later I wake up to Luke carrying Michael into the room. "What a perfect sight to see my two boys as I wake up," I say with a smile.

Luke kisses me and hands me Michael. I sit up in bed for a while holding Michael in my arms. I decide to watch the news. Luke comes in with a tray of breakfast food. "Breakfast in bed? I could get used to this. You truly are something special."

"Trust me, you're worth it," Luke says with his stunning smile. He takes Michael to his crib as we eat breakfast.

"Breaking news alert out of Denver, Colorado," I hear from the TV and my ears instantly tune in. "Luke, turn it up!"

The story is about the plane! The police stopped the men

before they got on the plane. They found the knife in their pocket. "Why hasn't Fredrick called me, dammit? If it were Tom, I'd have already known before the news." Then I stopped myself when I realized I just said his name. "I can't believe I said that."

"Me neither. But even though Tom was a killer, he was a good detective." I shake my head in disgust.

The pretty blonde newscaster explains more of the story. "The Denver Police wouldn't say much about the situation, but I do know that two detectives from Charleston, South Carolina are here on the premise as well. They are somehow involved. How did the police know that these men were going to attack? There are questions floating in the air at this point, but we are all glad that everyone is safe. More information and news to follow."

I look at Luke. "Sooner or later, they're going to put the pieces of the puzzle together, especially if I keep having major dreams like these. They're going to keep asking the hows, whys, and eventually, who. I don't know if my name will stay hidden."

"Let's take it one step at a time. You just saved hundreds of people's lives. If your name comes out at some point, we'll deal with it. There's no need to stress about it now."

"You're right. It does feel good to be a hero. Maybe my dreams have changed. I had one last night where I was on a cruise! It was a nice, relaxing dream. I'm sure there'll be more to it at some point."

The phone rings as Luke and I discuss the dreams. "Fredrick, why didn't you tell me you caught them sooner! I had to find out through the news."

"I know, I'm sorry. I tried to call sooner, but I was bombarded with questions. The good news is that everyone is safe. The bad news is I don't know if this will be enough information to put them away. We only found knives on them and of course none of them are giving up any information, which means if there are no prior crimes on their record, they'll walk free."

"What?" I yell into the phone. "That can't happen. They'll only do this again and next time they could succeed!"

"I know, I know, but we didn't have much information on them when we came in. We just went with what you told us. We didn't have names or anything. They're going to take their fingerprints and run them through the system. Let's keep our fingers crossed that they find out something."

"Oh God, I hope so."

"Arnold and I are going to stay until they find out more information about these men. I'll be in touch."

"Thanks." I hang up and sigh.

Luke rubs my back, "You did what you could, and it's out of your hands now. It's a beautiful day out. How about we go for a short walk with Michael? It'll do you good to get out of the house. Plus, it would be nice to have a relaxing day before I go back to work tomorrow."

"Do you have to go?" I say with a childish tone. "I've been spoiled with having you around all day."

"I know, babe. I've enjoyed it too, but it's time to go back to work."

"I'm going to be so bored! I'm only resting for one more week then I'm going back to work as well."

"As long as you're feeling stronger, you can start by working a few hours, so you don't overdo it."

"Yes, doctor," I say jokingly.

"Let's walk down to my coffee shop! I know Sarah and Bobby are dying to see Michael, plus it's not too far to walk."

"Sounds like a good plan." I put Michael in my carrier that's wrapped around the entire front side of my body. We walk down Rainbow Row. I feel like it has been decades since I've seen these beautiful colors, and the way the sun shines on these homes makes them look even more vivid.

I walk into the shop and the smell of coffee overtakes all of my senses. "Mmm, I've missed this smell."

I hear a loud screeching voice coming from Sarah, "OH MY GOODNESS, look who it is!" Bobby peeks his head out from the back. He's wearing an apron covered in flour.

"Linda, Luke, it's so good to see you," hollers Bobby. They both storm over.

"Look how cute Michael is! Oh my God, he's so adorable," Sarah says as he touches his cheek.

"He has a good mixture of the both of you," says Bobby. Even though Bobby is straight muscle, he does have a soft side to him.

"Thank you both, we're very happy." I look around at the full shop. Some of my regulars came up to us to talk as well.

I miss it here so much. I can't wait to get back to work. We sit around a leather circle couch in the shop and have coffee and talk about everything that has been going on. Sarah leaves periodically to help customers. "When can you come back to work?" Bobby asks.

"Hopefully in a week! But I'll have to start slowly until I'm 100 percent better."

"You better take it slow. The good thing is Sarah and I will be here to help you and Michael out."

"I'm very lucky to have the two of you."

Sarah walks back over after ringing up a customer, "Bobby and I have a surprise for you," she says as she holds out her hand for me to take.

I grab it and get up. "A surprise? What is it?" I say with excitement.

"Come with me and I'll show you." Sarah and Bobby walk me to our employee room. This is where our lockers are, plus there's a nice comfy couch to relax on throughout the day. I walk in, shocked at what I see. It's a brand new wooden crib, with Michael engraved on the side, and an animal mobile hanging above it. Tears immediately fall from my eyes.

"Oh you guys, this is amazing. You didn't have to do this." I walk over and touch the crib. There's a blue knitted blanket inside.

"We knew that you'd want to come back to work, and would have Michael, so we had this made for you so you have a place for him at our shop. He's now a part of our family as well," Sarah says with a big smile that lights up her face.

I hug them both as I wipe the happy tears away. "Words can't describe how happy I feel right now. Thank you both so much. Michael will fit right in!"

We stay for a little while longer, leaving when it's time to feed Michael. "We better get back. Thanks again for everything. I'll see you both in about a week! Love you both."

I lie in Luke's arms thinking about our day. I'm so thankful for everything. I yawn and close my eyes.

It's dark outside. The stars look so much bigger and brighter over nothing but ocean. I sit on the main deck of the ship and enjoy the sights of nature. BOOM! I fall out of my chair, my ears are ringing, and the ship is shaking and making a rumbling noise. I look up to a sky full of smoke. I hear screams and cries. I slowly get up and turn towards the middle of the ship. There's nothing but fire and smoke, and people running past me on the deck. I can't see the other side of the ship, but I imagine it's full of panicking people.

I try to stop someone as they run past. "What happened?"

"Something on the ship must have blown up. There's no land around us, and this boat won't last. What are we going to do?" the man says, crying as he runs away from me.

The ship won't last? Does he mean the ship is going to sink?" I get up, heart pounding. I try to breathe, but my breaths are heavy and short. I start to feel lightheaded.

I look over the railing and see a huge hole in the middle of the ship. The entire ship is cracked down the middle. The fire is starting to spread. Either the ship is going to burn first, or it's going to sink. Either way we're all stuck out in the middle of the ocean with nothing to do and no place to go.

I start to feel faint and queasy. I see black speckles. I lose my balance and fall down.

Chapter 5

My body twitches at the fall and I wake up. I quickly sit up in bed, dripping sweat from my forehead. I try to catch my breath. "A cruise ship. So many people. Explosion. Fire." I can't seem to put together full sentences.

"It's ok, just take a deep breath," Luke says. I take big deep breaths and Luke grabs a cool wash cloth. He dabs my forehead and I finally start to calm down. "Do you want to tell me the story?" I nod my head. Then I hear Michael start to cry. I begin to get up. "Stop, I'll get him."

I sit with my head leaning back on the headboard. I close my eyes and visions of the burning boat run through me like a fast slideshow. My head pounds. Flashes of the bomb exploding and the screaming people won't stop. I put my hands on the side of my head and close my eyes tight. "Stop!" I yell out in agony.

The sight of Michael immediately calms me down. I smile when he looks into my eyes. I begin to tell Luke the story.

"A cruise ship?" Luke asks.

"Yes, this is way bigger than the airplane dream. Think of all the people." Luke takes Michael and stands, bouncing him as he paces around the room.

"A bomb? This sounds like another attack. Why would anyone target a cruise ship?"

"Think about it, Luke. It's the perfect scenario; hundreds of people, a big ship out in the middle of the ocean, no land in sight."

He nods in agreement. "I guess you're right. Did you get a look at the name of the ship, or the company cruise line?"

I lower my head. "No, nothing, just the disaster, the same as the plane crash. It was horrible. I know this is bad to say, but at least the plane crash was a fast death and no one could see it coming. With the cruise ship, people are panicking the entire time, waiting for rescues that may never arrive."

"Come on now, it's not like the Titanic. I'm sure coastguard will help as soon as it happens. The technology has changed a lot since the Titanic."

"True, but what if the Captain is in on it and decides not to let anyone on the outside know what happened? What if he takes the ship off course so it'd be hard to locate?"

"Still, the company has GPS on the ship. They'd be able to find it. It may take longer, but there shouldn't be as many deaths as you think."

"Well any scenario will result in too many deaths. This has to be stopped, and I'm the only one who can stop it."

Luke takes Michael back to his crib. He brings me to him and I snuggle in his arms, head near his chest. "Just relax, babe. It's three in the morning, so try and get some sleep. We can figure this out tomorrow."

I lie there with my eyes shut trying to fall back asleep. *Why? Why such a big disaster? Why does this have to happen to me?* I begin to count backwards from one hundred, hoping that will help me fall back asleep.

I wake up to Luke's alarm tone, Eye of the Tiger. "Oh Luke, you seriously have to get a new alarm tone."

"No way, babe. It helps get me up and ready to take on the day! You're stuck with it," he says kissing me on the forehead. "Are you going to be ok here at home while I'm at work?"

"Yes, I promise. If I get lonely or feel anything coming on, I'll call Mom. She won't hesitate to come over."

"Ok, good."

Luke eats a bagel with cream cheese and drinks his coffee, while I feed Michael. "Want me to cook you something?"

"No, I don't really have an appetite. I keep picturing that ship in my head."

"I'm sorry, Linda. I hate that you have to go through this."

"Thanks, I'm just going to have to get used to it I guess."

"Do you have any plans you want to accomplish today?" Luke says with his mouth full of bagel.

A small smile grows on my face. "Yeah, I'm going to research all the different cruise ship lines and the boats. I want to see if I can find the ship that was in my dream. I know it's a long shot because a lot of ships look the same, but I'm hoping to eliminate a few."

"Sounds good. That might help you get more details when you dream about it again."

"Yep, that's my goal."

I walk Luke out the door and give him a kiss. "Have a great day back at work."

"Thanks, and if you need anything please call."

I decide to turn on the TV. If I'm lucky there'll be a marathon of Law and Order on. I make some coffee and take my laptop to the couch. I get comfy and ready to find out some information.

I start by researching Carnival Cruise, the most popular cruise line. As I read information I hear a knock on the door. *I wonder who that is?* I think to myself.

I cautiously walk towards the door and look through the peephole before opening it. "Fredrick, come on in!" I glance to each side wondering where Arnold is. "Where's your better half?" I ask jokingly.

"He's working on a case at the station. I wanted to take a break and come see how you were doing."

I lead him into the kitchen and pour him a cup of coffee. "Well, that's nice of you, thank you for checking up on me." *Is it ok that my new partner whom I don't know real well wants to check up on me? Stop, he's not Tom. This is a different situation; don't read too much into it.* I tell myself.

"How was the experience in Denver?"

He takes a gulp of his coffee. "Well it wasn't a pleasant one. The switch up at the end was a nail-biter, but in the end it all worked out for the best."

"And all the questions?"

"I got asked all the questions I was preparing for. How did you know they were here? How do you know they were going to attack the plane? Things like that. All the detectives and cops were puzzled at the situation, but eventually gave up and left it alone."

I sigh with relief. "Well that's good."

He looks at me intensely, like he has something important to say. "Ok, so I guess I'm not a good liar." My heart begins to beat faster. *Oh God please don't let it be what I think.* "I didn't just come here to see how you were doing. I came here because Arnold and

I need your help on another case."

A wave of relief instantly takes over. Thank goodness; I don't think this will be anything like the situation with Tom.

"Ok, what's the case?" I don't bother bringing up the cruise ship dream yet, because I don't want to get him all worked up. He seems to get stressed easily.

He takes out three folders from his black leather briefcase. "It's a pretty tough case." He opens one folder of a man. He is bald, with a smooth face, almost black eyes, and a long square nose. "This man was put in jail five years ago for multiple killings. Typical serial killer, he kills each woman in the exact same way. He'd drug the women, strip them of their clothes, and suspend them from the ceiling. He'd then burn them with cigarettes. Each woman had the burns in a straight line all the way down the middle of their body starting with the neck. He carved the letters WV on both wrists. He'd leave them there for two days, exactly 48 hours on the dot, and then stab them thirteen times to their death."

I swallow, and my heart starts to race. "That's awful." I feel faint.

"Are you ok? You don't look too good. Can I get you something?"

"Water please," I say as I lay my head on the table. I take small sips of the water and inhale big breaths.

"I'm sorry, this is all probably way too much for you to handle right now."

"You were right about this being a hard case."

"Oh, I haven't got to the hard part yet." I look at him with my eyebrow raised. "Are you ok for me to go on?"

I take another sip of water and nod my head in agreement.

"Well, this man," as he points to the bald man, "his name is Wilfred Valentine and I put him away five years ago for these crimes. The problem is, two women have been found dead with the exact same markings and same number of stabbing wounds. He targeted the same kind of women; all 25, blonde, and single. Either I've put the wrong man in jail, or there's a copycat out there."

"Fuck, talk about a major case."

"Yeah, and this is why we need your help desperately."

"Ok, it's going to be a real hard one to dream about and get through, but I don't want any more women to suffer this awful abuse and death."

"Would it help if I show you the two recent women who died? You can get a sense of what they looked like and what the markings looked like."

"I honestly don't want to see these pictures, but the more details the better." I brace myself before I look at the images. "Oh my God," I say in disgust. Tears begin to form and my stomach turns. Both women have long blonde hair, eyes shut, a blue tint to their lips, and pale skin. There are round burns down the middle of their bodies and thirteen stab wounds all over. "I think I'm going to be sick." Fredrick fills up my glass of water.

"Need aspirin?"

"No, just water."

"Are you sure you're going to be able to handle this?" My fear turns to anger at the thought of what this man did to these women.

"Yes, I want this bastard caught. The only problem is, where in the hell am I supposed to start?"

"Well, he found these women leaving bars around the downtown area. He seemed to stalk them late at night after they'd already had a few drinks. He watches them during the night, and then follows them when they leave."

"Any specific bar?"

"I don't know. When I interrogated him five years ago, he said he liked to go to different bars."

"Ok, well at least we know he targets bars downtown at night. That's a start. It's better than nothing. I can put myself in that area at night in my dream." I stop to contemplate something. "WV, the initials he carved in their wrists, matches Wilfrid Valentine?" I say questionably.

"True, but I'm sure there are more men out there with the initials WV. If it's a copycat, he may use WV to throw us off track. His name might not contain those initials or else the real WV is still out there and Wilfrid Valentine is an innocent man."

"How can that happen? I mean, what about DNA?"

"DNA was only found on one of the victims. He claimed to have had consensual sex with her the night of her murder. At first he claimed that he didn't kill her. Then we found him stalking another blonde woman one night. We picked him up and I interrogated him for almost twelve hours. He's the only suspect we had and the only DNA linking to at least one victim. He confessed after twelve hours that he committed each crime and how he did it."

"Wow, so the real murderer could still be out there."

"That's what I'm afraid of. Honestly, I wish it was a copycat, because if it's the same murderer from five years ago, he knows what he's doing, and he knows how to clean. We never got evidence of another male, not even a hair. How weird and freaky is that?!"

"That's definitely unusual. This is going to be tough."

"I appreciate your help."

"You're welcome, but after all that information I feel like I need a shot of patron or something." He laughs. "What, is that a laugh I hear from Detective Fredrick?"

"Every once and a while I break. I promise when we catch this guy, a shot of patron will be the perfect celebration."

"Sounds great." I begin to hear Michael crying.

I walk over and pick up Michael from his crib. "Well I don't want to bother you any longer. Thanks again for the help. Please keep me posted. If I find out any more information about this case I'll call you."

"Thanks Fredrick. I'll keep you posted every day until this is over."

He nods his head, smiles, and walks out the door.

I sit on the couch with Michael. "Phew, what a case mommy has on her hands," I say.

I look over at my laptop and see the cruise ship I had been researching. "Shit," I say out loud. I forgot all about that dream. My brain is already full of so much information. I need to concentrate on this serial killer case first. Maybe the cruise ship dream will come to me, but for right now I need to focus on whoever WV is, who he'll attack next, and how to stop him.

***

I decide to cook dinner for Luke. I'm going to make a chicken parmesan casserole. As the casserole is baking Luke walks in from work. "Hey babe, I missed you today. I became spoiled having you around all day," I say as I give him a kiss.

"I missed you too, and wow, something smells good in here," he says as he sniffs the air and walks into the kitchen.

"How was your day at work?"

"It was good. I had a few knee surgeries and one ankle. Everyone at the hospital is dying to meet you."

"You know it's crazy that after all this time I still haven't met some of the people you work with, except for crazy Jeff."

He chuckles. "Jeff doesn't stop talking about you. If he weren't my best friend I wouldn't be surprised if he tried to make his way in."

I smile. "I'm flattered, but Jeff seems like a player to me."

"Why do you think that? Is it because he has an outgoing personality? That he's very built? That he talks about how much he loves women? Actually you and many other people are wrong. He's one of the nicest and most loyal people I know. He was in a five year relationship and was going to ask this woman to marry him. He walked in on her in bed with another man. His heart was broken. He treated that girl like a princess. So he has trust issues."

"Wow, poor Jeff. Well, you just talked him up a bunch. Maybe I should make a move on him," I say with a wink. "Just kidding babe, you know you're the only one for me."

"I'd kick Jeff's ass!" We laugh. "But Jeff does want to stop by and see how you're doing some time."

"Tell him he's welcome here whenever. And when I'm able to go back to work, I'll have to come by the hospital to meet everyone."

"Perfect. Now let's dig into this amazing casserole," Luke says, licking his lips. "So how was your day? Did you get a lot of research done?"

"Sort of."

"Were you able to shorten the list of cruise lines?"

"No, Fredrick came by to see me."

"Oh?" Luke says with discomfort.

"He and Arnold need help with a case. It's a pretty serious one, and I have to help them. What this man does i...is horrible." I say with a gulp.

"What's the case?"

"We should finish eating before I explain it. You might lose your appetite. I know I will and I'm starved."

"Ok babe." We finish eating quickly and in silence. I can tell Luke is anxious to hear about the case. I've never seen him eat so fast in my life.

I swallow my last bite of the spicy, tangy casserole and begin to tell the story. Luke sits there with wide eyes, staring at me with shock as I go into detail of the torture.

"Are you sure you can handle this?"

"At first I didn't think I could. I almost passed out when Fredrick showed me the pictures and explained everything, but then the fear turned into anger. This man needs to be stopped before more sweet and innocent women die a gruesome death."

"You're one brave woman, Mrs. Jackson."

I smile. "Thank you. I'm going to focus tonight and try and get some information. I'm going to put myself downtown at around 10:30pm. That seems to be when the bars start to get busy. I'm going to try one bar and if it doesn't work I'm going to keep trying until I find him. I know it's a long shot, but it's better than nothing."

"You know I'll be here when you wake up."

"That means the world to me," I say as I give him a deep kiss that seems to linger.

I put Michael in his crib and do my nightly routine. As I lie in bed I start focusing, taking deep breaths, closing my eyes, and tuning everything out. Luke slowly gets under the covers on his side of the bed.

I open my eyes and he props up on his elbow and stares me in the eyes. "You know, I can do something to help you relax. It might help with the dreams," he says with a sexy grin.

"Oh yeah, and what might that be?"

He starts to kiss my lips softly. He moves his lips from mine and softly runs his mouth over my ears. I feel his light breath and the sensation is warming and satisfying, making my body sensitive all over. He starts to kiss my neck and slowly moves his body on top of mine. It seems like it has been forever since we have had sex, and oh how I've missed it.

He stops as he kisses my stomach. "Are you ok with this? It's not too soon is it? I mean how are you physically feeling?"

I smile at his dramatic worried feeling. "Babe I'm fine, I promise. I've missed this, and it's exactly what I need."

He smiles and whispers into my ear, "Ok good, I'm going to make you feel so good. Just lie back, relax, and let me take care of you."

God, I love it when he takes control. He's so soft with me,

I can tell he doesn't want to hurt me. "Babe, I'm not glass, I promise I won't break."

He bites my lip. "Good, because I don't like being this soft."

I bite his lip back. "Then don't be."

He looks at me as he spreads my legs wide open. We kiss deeply as he slowly enters me. When we start to get a rhythm going he looks at me and says, "Are you ready?"

"Oh yeah." He pushes hard and fast. My hands are back behind me pushing against the headboard. After a few minutes, I push him over and get on top. I ride him fast and hard. Watching him with his head back and eyes closed and moaning makes me ride even harder. I love that I can make him feel this good. Then he flips me back over, puts my legs on his shoulders, and moves in and out so fast. Faster and faster, sweating, tension building up, faster, harder, until I scream out with pleasure. He lets out a big moan then gently pulls out and lies on top of me.

I rub my hands through his damp hair and kiss him on the forehead. "Wow, that was amazing. I missed that so much. No more resting for me!" I say with a smile.

He kisses my lips softly. "Let's wait and see how you feel tomorrow. I want to make sure you're alright."

"Oh trust me, I am. I feel better than ever."

I lie on his chest and we talk about random things. I really needed this. No stress and no worries.

I yawn and feel my eyes become heavy. "Well, you should sleep well tonight. I hope I helped relieve some stress and make it easier to focus on the dreams."

"Oh, I'll sleep like a baby. I haven't felt this relaxed and stress free in a while. Thank you, Luke."

"Any time babe, day or night," he says with a soft smile.

I roll over onto the other side and close my eyes. It's time to find out some information.

I'm walking around downtown trying to find a bar. I'll start with one of the most popular, The Pavilion. I walk in and have no idea what to look for or who to look for. I guess I'll pay close attention to blonde women and any suspicious looking men. Oh boy, I didn't realize how hard this was going to be.

On this rooftop at night is nothing but loud dance music playing and men and women dancing. Surely this guy wouldn't do anything out in the open. Maybe I should wait on the streets and see if I find any strange men following women with blonde hair.

I head back to the front of Pavilion and back onto the street. It's still early so all I can do is walk around and wait. I have a habit of checking my phone to pay attention to the date and time. Today is Saturday on a warm summer evening on July 18th. Shit, that's this coming Saturday. I need to find information fast.

I walk up and down King Street many times. If people are watching me they probably think I'm crazy. I decide to walk down Bay Street. I know there are a few nice bars on that street. From a distance I can see the Bay Street Biergarten and decide to walk towards that bar. When I'm about a street away I see a pretty, tall, long blonde-haired woman in a tight red dress walking out. Then, a few seconds later I see a man walk out and follow closely behind her, but not too close that she'd notice.

This may be him! There's no way I can get this lucky first time around. I follow close behind the man. From behind he seems like an average male, dressed in dark blue jeans and a grey and white plaid shirt. He has brown boots on and his hair is a light brown color. No one would ever suspect him of being a killer, especially as malicious as the one who killed all those women. He starts to gain some speed on this girl. I have a feeling he's getting ready to attack. I try to pick my pace up and keep up with him. As I do so, I run straight into a trash can! "Oh shit," I whisper. I wasn't paying any attention to where I was walking. Fuck, I hope he didn't hear me. I look up and the man and woman have both gone!

"No, no don't do this to me! I was so close." Of course talking to myself isn't going to help much. I decide to keep walking that path to see if I can hear or see anything. As soon as I turn the corner onto Chapel St. someone grabs me from behind and puts his hand over my mouth as I try to scream out. He drags me into an alleyway so no one can see. I shake and squirm trying to free myself from his strong grip.

"You're not going anywhere," he says with a grunting, deep, eerie voice. I panic as tears run down my face. He shoves me hard up against a building wall and slaps me across the face with the back of his hand.

I feel an instant sharp pain in my face. I put my hand to my cheek and he grabs me by the neck. He looks deep into my eyes. "And who do you think you are to follow me? Why are you following me?" he says with whiskey on his breath.

I try to shake my head in disagreement and talk, but I can't breathe and can barely move. He loosens his grip a little. "I wasn't following you. I, I was just walking around trying to find a place to get a drink."

A small smile appears on his short bearded face, "Oh come on, do I look that stupid? Why are you following me?"

"Honestly I wasn't." BAM! Another blow to my face, this time with his fist.

"Better start telling me the truth or I'll keep punching until you can no longer move." My mouth is shut, and I'm frozen with shock. My head is pounding and face is aching, I can't concentrate on anything right now. BAM, BAM, more blows to my face left and right. I can't stand anymore and I cripple to the ground. He crawls on top of me. "You're not really my type, I prefer hot blondes, but I guess you'll do. I can't have you running off and telling the police who I am."

No matter what I say to him, he's going to kill me like he did the others. I have no choice and no way out. I pray to God that I wake up before I experience any of it. BAM, another hit to the face. I start to black out. My mind is fading and my body is becoming numb. He's taking my pants off as I fade away. "Please Linda, wake up," I whisper at the last moment, then nothing but darkness.

I wake up slowly. My body feels like its weighing down into the bed, like I have been beaten. I slowly open my eyes and begin to cry. I feel like I can't move. "Luke, Luke what's wrong with me?"

He quickly sits up in bed, turns on the light, and comes over to me. "Babe, what's wrong? Was it a dream?"

"Yes, but I feel like I can't move." I start to panic, and breathe heavily, as sweat forms on my forehead.

"Relax, relax. Here let me help you up." He puts his arms around my back and neck and drags me to sit upright against the head board. "What do you feel like? Do I need to call 9-1-1? Talk to me, Linda."

Tears fall. "I don't know. I had a horrible dream and was beaten almost to death, and now I can't move. My body feels numb."

"Fuck, I'm calling for an ambulance." He starts to get up.

"No wait. How in the hell would I explain this to anyone? Just give me some time. I'm sure it'll pass, like my headache and visions pass."

"Those only last for seconds, but this seems to be lasting longer."

"Just wait, please. Sit here with me and talk to me." I slowly start to move my fingers and toes. "I'm starting to get some movement and feeling back."

"How are you so calm about this?" he asks.

"Do you see my face right now? Lots of tear tracks. Waking up unable to move is the scariest thing I've ever experienced."

"The dream did this to you. This needs to stop. What if you actually became paralyzed from this?"

"I guess it was the dream. I mean, there's no other explanation."

"Why did this dream affect you so much worse than the others?"

"Because I was actually getting beaten in the dream, which must take a toll on my body. But it never did that before. Before I had the coma, when I was beaten in my dreams, I never experienced anything like this. I'm scared. I don't know what's going on with me." I cry some more as I begin to move my legs and arms.

"Linda, this isn't right. We need to do something."

"You're right Luke, it isn't right. I've had enough of this, but who can we talk to?"

"I know you might think it's crazy, but I'm thinking some sort of witch doctor or psychic?"

"That does sound crazy. I'm not sure if they're even real, but it's worth the research. I know if we go to a real doctor they'll put me away in a hospital somewhere."

"That's exactly what we want to avoid."

"I can't believe this is happening to me."

"I know, I'm so sorry baby." Michael begins to cry over the monitor. I feed him and discuss my dream with Luke.

"You'll have to call Fredrick first thing in the morning," says Luke with concern.

"I know. Good thing is we know where and when he's going to attack. I have a visual of what he looks like and the woman he may attack. I hope catching him will be as easy as we think."

"I hope so too, and you won't go anywhere near that scene!"

"I wouldn't dare. I wouldn't put myself in such danger."

"Good, finally we agree for once." Michael falls back asleep lying on my chest. I hold him for a while. Luke has his arm around the both of us as we relax and talk about everything but dreams.

It feels good lying here with both of my boys. We have such a nice little family. I hope my dreams don't ruin what a wonderful life we have. I've been scared before, but after what I experienced tonight I've never felt so afraid, worried, and stressed than I do now. These dreams are starting to affect my body and my health. Now when I have dreams, not only do I have to worry about trying to find information out, but also about how badly it's going to hurt me, and how far it will go.

Chapter 6

I wake up the next morning to the sound of Luke's alarm. I rise out of bed slowly. "Wow, I don't even remember falling back to sleep last night."

Luke yawns. "Both you and Michael were fast asleep in my arms. It was an amazing moment for me. I put him back in his crib before I fell asleep again."

I get out of bed. My body feels sore, as if I did an entire body lifting workout. Luke can see me struggling. "Body still hurts?" I nod in agreement. "Are you going to be ok today alone again?"

"Yes, I promise. I'm going to call Fredrick and give him the details and then probably do more research about the cruise ships. I can't wait to get back to work next week."

"I'm sure you can't, babe."

I put on a pot of coffee while Luke is getting ready for work. I grab my phone and call Fredrick. "Helloooo, this is Fredrick's phone. He's currently away from the phone because he's sitting on the Jon." I smile at the sounds of Arnold's childish voice.

"Hey Arnold," I say with a laugh.

"Hey there Linda, I knew it was you calling. I wouldn't have done that if it was someone else."

"I know that. You made me laugh, which is exactly what I needed."

"Great! Oh shit, here comes the boss man."

I hear a scuffle over the phone. "What are you doing answering my phone calls?" I hear Fredrick saying to Arnold.

"Sorry dude. I saw it was Linda and didn't think you-"

"Ugh," sighs Fredrick into the phone. "I'm sorry about that, Linda. He can be too immature sometimes."

"No, no don't be sorry. He made me laugh."

"Well I guess he's good for some things," he says jokingly. "I hope you're calling for some good news?"

"Yes and no. I had a terrifying dream last night and found out some information about the killer."

"Ok, I'll come by to get some information and bring my sketch artist."

"No, I want to get out of the house. I'll come down to the station. I'll drop off Michael with my Mom."

"Ok, come down and we'll grab some lunch and talk."

"Sounds great, see you soon," I say as I hang up the phone.

"Be careful going down there today," Luke says as he pours his coffee into this travel coffee mug."

"I will babe, don't worry."

He hugs me tightly and kisses me with passion. "Last night was really good."

I smile. "Yes it was, can't wait to do it again," I say with a wink.

"Have a good day, beautiful," he says as he walks out the door.

I give Mom a call. Luckily she's off work today and will gladly take care of Michael for a little while, which I knew she'd agree to.

I walk into the station. It's full of black cop uniforms; people roaming around, the sound of computers typing, the sound of people talking, and the smell of coffee.

I wave to Fredrick and Arnold sitting at their corner desk. Arnold has his big goofy smile on. "Hey! Glad to see you out and about," says Arnold.

"Thanks, it feels good to be out of the house."

"Before we head to lunch, I want you to describe the man to my sketch artist as best as you can," says Fredrick.

I nod in agreement. The artist has a pad and pencil and continues to draw as I speak the details. "He's around 6 feet tall. He walks with a small hunch. He was wearing blue jeans and gray plaid shirt. He has a short beard, dark eyes. I couldn't really tell the color because it was night. His eyes seemed pretty wide, in an eerie and crazy way. He had a cleft chin, and had short dark hair."

Once the sketch artist has finished drawing he shows me the man. My stomach instantly turns. "Wow, that looks just like him." The picture brings back the images of him beating me. As the picture flashes in my head, I instantly feel pain. I close my eyes and rub my head.

"Linda, are you ok?" asks Fredrick.

"Ye…yeah. Just a headache." He grabs a painkiller and water and hands it to me.

"Thank you."

"You're welcome. So how about we head to the Park Café for lunch?"

"Sounds good to me!"

"Me too. They have awesome sandwiches," Arnold shouts with excitement.

Fredrick drives as we begin to discuss the case. I tell them which bar it took place at and how I found them. We pull into the parking lot and head inside. I order the House Smoked Ham Melt Sandwich. We get our meals and grab a bench outside.

"You said the dream was terrifying?" asks Fredrick.

I swallow a bite of my sandwich and take a breath. "Yeah, he caught me following him, grabbed me, and beat me practically to death. I woke up before anything else happened."

"I'm so sorry," says Fredrick. Arnold nods along with him.

"What's worse is that this dream seemed to affect my body when I woke up. I couldn't move and didn't get any feeling back until after a while. My body is also sore as if I'd really been beaten. I'm scared to death. My dreams have never done this to me before."

"And the headache at the precinct?"

"Yes, I get flashes from my dreams and an abrupt pain in my head, which feels like a stabbing knife."

"Hmm, that's strange," says Fredrick. "Maybe these cases are just too much for you now. I don't want to be responsible for bringing this pain upon you."

"It's not you. No matter what I do I'll have a dream. I can't stop them. They're just somehow escalating into my waking life. Luke and I are stuck on what to do. We know a real doctor would think I'm crazy and then he mentioned a witch doctor or something."

Fredrick looks at me then at Arnold and they give each other an informative look with their eyebrows raised.

"What is it?"

"Well my aunt is a psychic who practices magic. She puts together all her own herb medicine mixtures, she reads palms, reads tarot cards, practices spells, and holds séances. She's a loony, but seems to know what she's doing," says Arnold.

"No way! Wow, I'm lucky because Luke and I were going to try to find someone in Charleston. Could I meet with her?"

"Yes, absolutely. She loves helping people and will love it even more if I bring her someone who needs help. It'll be a sense of fulfillment for her."

"Great, thank you so much."

"How about I take you on Friday evening? She likes working at night better; she thinks she gets better readings at that time."

"Perfect, I'll tell Luke. Ok, now what are you going to do about Saturday?"

"Well, we have a good amount of information so it shouldn't be hard to catch this guy. We'll have officers surrounding the area undercover. When we see the woman and man with the description you give us then we'll attack."

"Sounds easier said than done. I remember how that worked. The bad guy somehow always seemed to get away."

"Linda, we aren't Tom. Remember all those men were working for him. We want to catch the killers and put them away."

"You're right, I'm sorry. I guess it still freaks me out a little."

"Don't be sorry. That's something that's very hard to overcome."

We finish eating our lunches. Once we get back to the station, I head to my Mom's to pick up Michael. On my way there my phone rings. Surprisingly it's Luke. Usually I hardly hear from him while he's at work because he's always so busy. "Hey babe, what a nice surprise!"

"Hey, I'm just calling to check in on you."

"Well aren't you sweet. I'm doing fine, just met with Fredrick and Arnold. Oh, and I've got some good news about a witch doctor. I'll tell you about that over dinner."

"Great! I'll pick up some food from Mellow Mushroom, if you want to call it in around 6:00?"

"Yum, that sounds good. I'll do that. See you in a little bit. I love you."

"I love you, too."

***

Arnold picks us up in his Toyota 4Runner at 7:00pm on the dot. "Thank you again for doing this for me," I say as I close the car door.

"Don't mention it. She's good at what she does and I'm hoping that you'll leave with some useful information."

"Thank you, me too."

We pull into a gravel driveway. In front of me stands an A-framed shape house made of brown bricks. The windows are outlined in brown and white wood. This sure looks like a house that belongs to a witch or psychic.

"Prepare yourself when you walk in, as she likes to go a little overboard with this stuff," says Arnold with caution.

I glance at Luke with an unsure look. We walk into a smell of spiced incense. The lights are off and candles are lit through the entire house. There's a round table set up in the living room with four chairs. Sitting in the middle of the table is a large, round white candle. There are dangling beads hanging over each doorway. The walls are painted a dark purple. He wasn't kidding about her going all out.

"Welcome, welcome," says a deep monotone woman's voice. I look over and see her walking through the hanging beads. Her long navy blue and purple dress flows as she enters into the room. I look into her dark eyes covered with too much make up, as I shake her hand.

I try to fake a smile, "Hello, I appreciate you taking the time to see me."

"Oh honey, it's my pleasure," she says as she shakes her head; her oversized half-moon earrings dangle with her movements "Everyone please come and have a seat and we shall get started." *Get started on what?* I think with a little fear of the unknown.

We all sit on the padded chairs. She closes her eyes, takes a deep breath, and shakes out her hands. It's hard to concentrate with her overwhelming curly hair in front of me. Ok, Linda, please tell me what has been going on with you."

I explain my whole story from the beginning of how my dreams started, to my coma, and how the dreams have affected my health.

Her eyes stay shut the entire time I'm explaining the story. "Mmhm I see," she says with a whisper. She grabs my hands and as soon as she touches me, what feels like a bolt of electricity runs through the both of us. We both jump back and let out a big breath.

"What the heck was that?" I say with a shortness of breath. Luke rubs my back for comfort.

"You have a very strong presence and aura about you."

"What's that supposed to mean? Why do these things happen to me?"

"You have a very precious gift, Linda. You have something inside you that no one else has that I've ever seen. It seems like during your coma your body went through a reconstruction. Your gift became more powerful than ever."

"Yeah, I pretty much knew that already. You're not telling me anything new." I start to get impatient. I'm sick of feeling this shock and pain.

"You're going to have to fight hard to control this gift, because it's affecting your body. It'll get better with time. There's no going back or getting out of the gift you hold. Strength and control is what it's going to take."

I put my head down. "Great, just great."

"Don't be down, Linda. You're special and magical. You're a hero. Mediating can help the situation. Try to relax and meditate at least once a day before you go to bed. Clear your head and put yourself in a relaxed state. This can help prevent the shock the dreams put on your body because when you're stressed and tense the outcome is much worse. If you're more relaxed, it won't affect you as much. When you get the shocking feeling or flashes, immediately close your eyes, take deep breaths, and concentrate on that darkness within your body and mind."

I nod my head up and down. "Ok, I can try and do that."

"But this is nothing I can fix, nor a real doctor. God gave you a gift, so embrace it, use it, and be empowered with it."

I start to feel a sense of fulfillment talking to her. I know I can't fix it now so it's time to put it past me, get over it, and start to have control. "Thank you so much, this really did help me out. I feel better mentally about it."

"You're more than welcome, my dear. Please call me if you have any troubles. If you seem to have trouble with the control let me know and I can whip you up some relaxing remedies."

"Sounds good, thank you."

I feel relief on the car ride back home. "Thanks again for taking us," I say to Arnold as we get out of the car.

Luke grabs my hand as we walk up to the front door. I turn

towards him and look into his eyes. "Babe, are you ok?"

I nod my head up and down. "For once I'm starting to feel ok with everything."

"Good, she was right as you're something special. You're a true gift."

"Thanks baby, now let's go inside and see our precious gift."

We walk in the door to Mom holding Michael in her arms. He's fast asleep. What a precious moment to encounter. Mom smiles with her big rosy cheeks. I walk over and kiss Michael softly on his cheek and carry him to his crib.

I walk back downstairs and Mom and Luke are already sipping a glass of wine. I smile and shake my head. "Thanks again Mom for watching him."

"Oh don't ever thank me. It makes me so happy to do it. So tell me about what happened, and I'll fill your Dad in when I get home."

I tell her the story as we all enjoy some wine.

***

I lie in Luke's arms as my eyes become heavy. The sound of Luke's heartbeat slowly sends me to sleep.

Screams everywhere, people panicking, fire bulging, the smoke is overwhelming. It's burning in my eyes and nose. I stand with my hands on the rails of the ship looking out into the middle of nothing but dark water. People are running past me, shoving me. Why panic when we know how this is going to end? The boat is going to sink and thousands of people are going to fight for their lives. So what should I do now? Wait until the ship goes down hoping maybe a coastguard can save us, or jump into the water and get it over with?

I start to think about why I keep having the dream in the same part, and why I'm not seeing the beginning. I have no idea where the hell this cruise ship is. As I become lost in transition, with thoughts of death and fear, a middle-aged man walks up next to me.

"Seems like you and me have the same idea about what's going on."

I look over at his salt and pepper hair and beard. "Oh yeah? What's your take on all this, and why aren't you freaking out like all the others?" Screams in the background start to fade, or maybe I'm just getting used to the screeching sounds.

"There's literally nothing we can do about this situation but wait. Why freak out and use up what energy we have to try and survive?"

"I completely agree. Either way, this isn't going to end smoothly."

"Glad I found someone who's sane," the man says with a small smile.

"This is going to sound strange, but where was this cruise headed and where did it leave from?"

He doesn't hesitate to answer or find it strange. "We left from the port out of Charleston, SC." Before he could finish his sentence a knot forms in my stomach. Charleston? Seriously, what a coincidence?

He continues, "And we were heading to Eastern Caribbean." I'm caught in a daze about this whole situation. The good thing is, I should be able to help stop it since it's taking off in our area.

"Ma'am, are you ok?"

I shake my head out of the daze. "Yes, I'm just a little shaken up."

He turns and looks back at the burning boat. "Yeah, aren't we all?"

I turn to face the flames. The ship is in chaos right now. All of a sudden the ship starts to shake and we have to grab onto the railing. "Shit, what's happening?"

"I think the ship is falling apart and filling with water quicker."

"Fuck, what are we going to do?"

"If we stay on the ship as it sinks, the undertow is going to be very strong and drag us under. It'll be hard to swim out of it. If we jump now and try to swim away as much as we can I think we have a better shot." Trembling profusely, I almost fall to my feet. My stomach is beyond the point of being nauseous but there's no point in puking as that will only make matters worse.

"THE SHIP IS SINKING!" someone yells as they run by. The screams seem to grow louder. People start jumping off the side of the boat. I glance around and see kids crying, holding onto their parents. No disaster like this should ever happen. I've got to stop this.

"Well, should we join the rest and jump?" the man asks me.

I take a deep breath. "I don't know if I can get the courage to jump, as I'm so scared." My heart is pounding out of my chest, my palms are sweaty, and tears engulf my eyes. "Wait!" I need to get this question out before the dream is over. "What day is it?"

The man looks at me with an eyebrow raised. "Today is July 17th and the cruise set sail on the 15th."

The 17th? No, this can't be. Tears begin to fall when I realize that I'm too late; thousands of lives have gone. I crumble to my knees *in agony. The man doesn't say anything, but I feel his glare on my back.*

I want to wake up from this dream. I stand up and jump over the rail into the water. The stinging sensation makes my body numb and I begin to sink.

I let out a big sigh and sit up quickly in bed. I begin to cough uncontrollably. I can't seem to catch my breath. Tears are falling, as I try to speak out. "Too…" more coughing "late."

"Linda, baby, relax." Luke brings me into his arms and holds me. "Shh, you're ok now." I start to relax a little and take big, deep, slow breaths. I close my eyes and breathe in and out through my nose. My heart is still pounding and my forehead is covered in sweat.

"What happened?"

"Turn on the news." Luke grabs the remote from the end table and turns it on. A breaking news story is on. "Turn it up," I say with fear.

The news is talking about a cruise ship that left from Charleston and got lost at sea. Coastguards are now scanning the areas the ship traveled. "Thousands of scared families are waiting to hear news about their loved ones, but how could a ship go missing?" the reporter stated. "We will be providing updates as often as we can."

"Your dream?" Luke asks me.

"My dream was too late. How could this be?"

He kisses my forehead. "I'm so sorry."

Tears run down my cheeks. To know what all those people went through and to know that I could have stopped it, is the worst feeling in the world. I roll over on Luke's chest, hold my stomach in pain, and cry.

Chapter 7

I stare blankly at the ceiling for the rest of the morning. Pictures flash through my head, shocking my body, causing sharp pains in my head. I have visions of the boat burning, kids crying, the woman in the red dress, the man beating me, so many flashes, so many shocks, so much pain.

"Ahhhh," I scream out. "Make it stop, it hurts so bad." I stumble off the bed and fall on my knees onto the floor. I grab my head and bend over, rocking back and forth.

Luke quickly runs to my side. "Control it, Linda, fight it, and find the strength." However, there's no strength inside me right now. All I feel like doing is giving up.

"Don't give up baby. You have to fight this."

Big deep breaths, come on Linda be strong, I say to myself. *Black everything out, complete darkness, envision the dark.* The pain and shock slowly starts to fade. My breathing becomes longer and more relaxed. I slowly lift my head. My face is sticky from the tears. I look into Luke's eyes and everything starts to become better.

He gently grabs my face with his warm hands and kisses my forehead. "I knew you could do it. You're so strong, Linda." He gently kisses my lips and wraps me in his arms. I'm finally relaxing in the arms of the man I love so deeply.

"You're my strength, Luke."

He kisses the top of my head and slowly rocks me back and forth.

We both walk into Michael's room and I pick him up. "He's our strength," Luke says. I smile and kiss Michael on the forehead.

"You're right about that." Luke heads down to make breakfast and I rock in the chair as I feed Michael.

I get lost in these moments when it's just Michael and I, and everything else seems to fade away. This is what I'm fighting for, my two favorite men. I put Michael in his carrier and walk around with him. I don't feel like letting go. I sit down to eat a wonderful breakfast with my family.

"Not only did I wake up to a horrible night, now I have to wait all day and night to see if this man shows up tonight and if it truly happens. Who knows now that my dreams are all out of whack?"

"Don't get discouraged, babe. It was only one dream."

"One very important dream that involved many lives."

"Let's try and have a relaxing Saturday. It's a beautiful day. Maybe we can take Michael to Waterfront Park."

"Sounds good to me," I say as I pick up the paper. The front page of the paper is about the missing cruise ship from Charleston, SC. I throw the paper down. Everywhere I turn for the next few weeks, there will be something about this ship, and all I'll be able to think about is how I could have stopped it.

"Linda, you can't hold something this big over your shoulders. It'll affect your stress level and health even worse than it already is."

"I know, I know," I say with a sigh. "It's hard not to think that though."

"I'm sure it is hard, and I wish I had the slightest of clue of how it feels."

"No you don't."

"Yes, I do, and then maybe I could find a way to help you."

"You do help me, Luke."

"How?"

"Just by being you, the support you give me, how much you care and love me, that's all I could ask for."

"And that will never stop, I can promise you that."

I smile at him as he gets up, walks over and kisses me, then grabs my plate to clean up.

"I can tell you one thing, I'm beyond ecstatic that I get to go back to work on Monday. I love that I can keep Michael with me at my job. How much better can it get?"

"Yeah, I'm already jealous that you've gotten to spend all day with Michael and now you get to spend it with him as you work! You've got the life, babe," he says with a smile.

"Yeah, I'll start off by working only half days so I don't overdo it."

"That's the smartest thing you've said. Usually you're stubborn and want to work, work, work."

I laugh. "Yeah, but it's different since I'll have Michael with me."

"Very true. So how about that walk to the park?"

"I think we're ready!"

It's a warm and sunny day in Charleston. We walk on the pier enjoying the sight of the blue-green water. We stop at the end and look out at the endless ocean. I close my eyes, take in the scent of the salt in the air, listen to the sounds of laughter, and feel the warm rays on my face. I take a deep breath in and out. This feeling, this moment is relaxing.

"Doing ok, babe?" Luke asks as I open my eyes to his beautiful blue eyes.

"Yes, I feel completely relaxed right now."

He smiles a beautiful tender smile. "Good, that's what I wanted for you." He kisses me on the forehead. I look down at Michael who can't seem to take his eyes off the glistening water.

"Looks like another one of us is relaxed," I say as I nod down towards Michael. We walk back towards the fountain as Luke's arm holds us close. I glance over at the fountain. I stop in my tracks when I see a man in blue jeans and a baseball cap pushed low over his eyes. My eyes begin to fill with tears instantly and my heart races. I shake my head as the tears fall. "No, no this can't be."

Luke stops and stands right in front of me. My vision of the man is now gone. "What Linda? What's wrong?"

"Over…" I can't seem to finish my statement. I point towards the fountain. Luke turns to face the fountain, opening the view for me again as well.

"What do you see, Linda?"

I look up in shock, but no one is there. Luke guides me to a bench to sit me down. I breathe in and out trying to control my breaths. I shake my head. "I must be seeing things, Luke. I know it must have been my imagination because there's no way what I say could exist."

"What did you see?"

"From a distance, I saw a man who looked exactly like Tom. He was wearing a low baseball cap so I couldn't see his eyes and blue jeans."

Luke's face immediately turns to a cold hard look. "He's in jail and he's not getting out. There's nothing to worry about, Linda. There are many men that wear those same clothes."

"I know, but the way he was standing, facing me seemed familiar." Luke looks over at the fountain again and begins searching the area. "But, you're right. It wasn't him, just my imagination I guess. These dreams are taking their toll on me."

Luke grabs my hand and stands Michael and I up. "Let's get you home to rest."

I nod in agreement as we walk. My heart is still pounding. *I mean there's no way Tom can get out of jail? I hope not. I've never been so scared. I've always been scared of Tom getting out and what would happen if he did. But the lawyer promised me he wouldn't. Ugh, snap out of it Linda. It was just a hallucination,* I say to myself trying to make myself feel a little better.

When we get home Luke makes some lunch meat wraps as I feed Michael. I keep replaying the man in my head. I try to stop but I can't help it. My thoughts redirect to the woman in the red dress. I hope Arnold and Fredrick can stop the man before anything happens. There are so many thoughts in my mind right now, it's making my eyes heavy.

Luke and I relax on the couch for a while watching some TV. Michael is fast asleep in my arms. My eyes start to close when we hear a knock on the door. Luke instantly gets up with concern. He walks towards the door slowly in an attack stance, like a wolf about to catch its prey. Another knock.

"Guys, open up. It's May." I sigh in relief and laugh. Luke laughs also and opens the door.

May comes storming in, her long brown hair swaying from side to side. "Jeez guys, what took so long? And why in the world is your door locked in the middle of the day?"

"Just precaution," I say.

She gives me a puzzled look. "Is everything ok?"

"Yeah. So what's up?"

"Nothing, I just wanted to come by and see my amazing nephew."

"Oh, I see how it is. You don't want to see your big sister anymore. What am I, chopped liver?" I say jokingly.

She winks at me and slowly lifts Michael as his eyes begin to open.

"If he starts to cry I'm going to kill you," I say as I yawn.

"Oh don't worry. Look at him. He's as calm as can be."

Luke chimes in, "So where is your better half?"

May gives a small grin. "Charlie is resting on the couch. He has been feeling a little sick the past few days."

"Sorry to hear that. How are things between the two of you? You seem to be really happy."

"I haven't been this happy in a long time. I really think he's the one."

I smile. "That's awesome, sis. Looks like you're going to be the next one to get hitched."

"Yeah, you never know," May says smiling. She asks how my dreams are. We discuss dreams and work, and she ends up staying for dinner.

I let her take some leftovers home to Charlie. "Thanks for stopping by, May."

"Of course, sis. Next time don't lock me out!" she says with a giggle. She struts out the door in her designer jeans and wedges. She's definitely the total opposite of me. I'd much rather lounge around in sweat pants. She can pull it off, though.

The time seems to be passing slowly today. This always happens when I hope for good news. It takes a lot out of me.

"Let's head to bed. We both know Fredrick won't call until the morning," Luke says as he gets up off the couch. He picks me up and carries me into the bedroom and gently lays me on the bed.

I look him in the eyes. "You spoil me, you know?" I say with a smile.

"I know I do, but that's ok, you deserve it." I smile and give him a soft kiss. He lies down next to me and wraps me in his arms.

It doesn't take long for my eyes to get heavy and begin to close. I try to clear my head of thoughts. Flashes of my dreams start to run through my head. I close my eyes tight. *Darkness Linda, think of darkness. Push these thoughts away, get the strength.*

I begin to ease my eyes into a relaxing state. The thoughts disappear, and I fade into the darkness.

***

I wake up to the sound of Michael crying in the monitor. "Well, I made it a few hours of dreamless sleep," I say to Luke. I feel pretty rested. I get up and walk into Michael's room.

57

After I'm done feeding Michael, Luke takes him and rocks him. "I'll take care of the rest, you get back to bed."

I wake up again to the sun shining through my blinds. I take a minute to enjoy a nice night's sleep, only to be interrupted by my phone ringing. I quickly grab it.

"Fredrick, please give me good news."

"Yes, good news. There was a woman in a red dress and the man matched your exact description. We caught him with her in the alley. He was just getting started with her when we stopped him. She's ok. Just a few bruises on her face and ribs. He's in our station now and we're going to start the interrogation. I want you to come down real quick to make sure this is the same guy you saw in your dreams."

"Ok, I can do that. I'll be there in twenty minutes."

"Great, see you then."

Luke looks over at me. "I'm guessing they want you to ID him?"

"Yup. The girl is ok, a few bruises but nothing as bad as it would have been if they didn't stop him."

"Good, I'm glad she's ok. Well we better get dressed and head down there. We'll grab some breakfast after."

I quickly get dressed and put Michael in his carrier. Luke drives us to the station. Arnold greets us with his childish hug and smile. "What's up guys?"

"Anxiously waiting to see this man; I sure hope it's the same guy from my dreams."

"Well follow me. Fredrick is with him in the integration room right now."

My heart pounds as we follow Arnold down the brightly lit hallway. He opens the door and I see the window in front of me. I walk closely up to the window and glare at the man. I look at details. His dark, wide eyes, cleft chin, and dark hair. I take a big gulp. "Y-yes that is him," I say with fear.

You'd think that after many times of seeing the killers in person rather than in my dreams I'd get used to the feeling, but nothing is more frightening than seeing a murderer in real life. Flashes shock through my head from the dream. BAM! Hit to the face by this man. I grab my head and place my hand on the wall as I stumble.

Luke places his hand on my back. I put both hands on the wall and close my eyes. *Fight it Linda, think darkness. Big deep breaths.* After a few minutes the flashes stop. "I think I'm starting to get the hang of controlling that!" I say with excitement.

Luke shakes his head and grins.

"Do you need water or anything?" asks Arnold. I shake my head in disagreement. Arnold knocks on the glass and Fredrick gets up out of his seat. I stare blankly into the eyes of the murderer.

"Is this the man?" Fredrick asks me.

"Yes it is. Did he admit to anything?"

He shakes his head in dissatisfaction. "No, he won't give up the previous murders and he says he has no idea who Wilfred Valentine is. This man's name is Chuck Archer and he has a really good poker face. He's viscous and he knows what he's doing. Before I could ask him any more questions he asked for a lawyer. For now he stays locked up because we found him in action beating the woman. Our DA is going to have to fight for this case. We have no DNA from the previous murders so it's going to be a tough case."

My hands shake and sweat. The look in his eyes is pure rage. "This man could be let loose. I'll try and help as well. Maybe I can find out more information with my dreams."

"Anything will help, Linda. We appreciate it."

"I'll be in touch." On the way home Luke plays the news on the radio and there's updated information on the missing cruise ship. They still haven't found the ship despite checking the route it was supposed to take multiple times. They're assuming the ship was abducted and taken off track and they're continuing the search.

I turn off the radio. "I can't hear any more about that ship. There's no way they're ever going to find it. It's long gone, at the bottom of the ocean now. Someone took it off track."

"I'm sorry, Linda." I sit there quietly thinking of all those innocent people. There's got to be something I can do.

The day seems to pass quickly. I start back at work tomorrow and I'm beyond happy to have something to do during the day. I lie in bed early to prepare for the work day.

I close my eyes and think of this Chuck man to see if I can find anything out. Maybe I get lucky enough to dream about him and receive more information on the cruise ship. If I can put myself before the explosion maybe I can search for some answers. I take a deep breath. There are so many answers and information that need to be found.

I'm standing near the fountain at Waterfront Park. I look around waiting to hear or see something I need to pay attention too. I sit on the edge of the fountain and watch closely. Suddenly I hear a man's voice behind me. I try to turn around but the sound of his voice has me frozen with fear. Chills instantly run down my neck and back from the fear of this familiar voice. "Linda, I'm watching you. Whether you like it or not I'm still here with you. I told you that you wouldn't be able to get rid of me. I'll be your nightmare, forever." The image flashes through my head from the other day at this park when I thought I saw the man in the baseball cap.

Tears flood my eyes. I turn to face the man who I hoped I'd never see again. No one is there, but the voice replays in my head, and only one word comes to mind: Tom.

Chapter 8

I wake up to Luke shaking me. "Linda, Linda wake up." I slowly open my eyes, and look right into Luke's watery eyes. "Oh, thank god you're ok."

I give him a puzzled look, confused at what's going on.

"It looked like you were having a seizure. Your body was shaking uncontrollably. Are you ok?"

I grab my head and close my eyes. "Yeah, I think I'm ok, it's just a headache." Then the images from the dream return to me. The sound of Tom's voice echoes through my mind and more tears fall.

"I'm assuming it was a dream that caused that shaking. What did you dream about?"

"You're not going to be happy about this. I still can't believe it happened."

"What was it, babe?"

"Tom came to me in my dream. I was at the fountain when I thought I saw him. I didn't see him in my dream but he talked to me. His voice sounded vindictive and mean." I tell Luke what he said.

"That fucking bastard! How is he doing this?"

"Remember he could see things in the future before they happened as well? I think he has found a way to get into my dreams. He wanted me to always remember him and now he has found a way to make that happen."

Luke's look changed from concern to anger. His cheeks turn red and his lips press together tightly. He abruptly flips up the covers and gets out of bed. He begins to pace around the room. "Something has to be done about Tom. I'm not going to let him do this to you. You had me scared to death when I tried to wake you up this morning."

61

I hesitate to answer, "W-well what if it was just a dream? I did freak out when I thought I saw him the other day. Maybe I only had that dream because I'm still scared from seeing him. Maybe there's no connection and it won't happen again."

Luke glances at me and shakes his head. "Nothing you say is going to make this better. I don't think this is a coincidence, especially what he said to you in your dream. I'm going down to talk to Fredrick. There's only one way to get rid of Tom for life." Silence takes over the room. "Death."

"Woah, Luke. You're talking about killing someone. That isn't how we solve issues. I won't let you get put into jail because of me."

"That's why I want to talk to Fredrick. There has to be a way to do this silently."

"He's in jail. There's no way you'd ever get away with this. Wait before you do anything, please. It might have been a fluke dream. Don't take any action, including talking to Fredrick without my consent. Wait and see if I have any more dreams first. If they continue then maybe we can talk to Fredrick together."

Luke continues pacing around the room shaking his head from side to side. He sighs in response. "Ok fine, but if you have one more dream that's it. I'm taking the next step because I'm not risking your health or state of mind. Tom isn't going to hurt you and get away with it."

I get up to feed Michael. As I leave the room Luke is sitting up in bed glaring at the wall. I hate to see him like this, as it scares me. I'm afraid he may take serious action. The thing I'm most afraid of is losing Luke because of a stupid mistake.

I crawl back into bed. Luke is already asleep. I kiss him on the forehead and turn to face my clock, which reads 3:30am. Hopefully I can get a few more hours of sleep before my first day back at work. I close my eyes when a chill runs down my back as Tom's voice plays over and over again in my head.

I find myself walking along the beach. The sun is setting and the soft sand beneath my feet feels captivating. I glance around and notice there are no people to be seen. I take a closer look and realize that I don't recognize this beach or area at all. This definitely isn't Folly Beach, so where am I?

I begin to feel anxious wondering what I'm about to walk into. It looks like a wall of rocks, almost like a maze. The adventurous side of me takes over and I walk around slowly to search for the rock maze. I walk up to one side, place my hands on the edge of the wall, and glance around. I see nothing but more rock and sand. I step into the maze of rocks and stop suddenly when I hear someone panting.

I slowly peek around another corner and see sand flying in the air. What the hell is going on?

I see a man in shorts and a tank top with a shovel. He's digging deep holes in the ground. I can't see his feet. I gulp when I see three more rectangle size holes, large enough to fit a body inside.

I notice the dark hair and build of this man, but I want to get a look at his face to make sure. His head is pointing towards the ground as he digs effortlessly, so I quickly prance behind another wall. I stand there with my back against the wall and my eyes shut, hoping he didn't hear me. I wait for a few minutes before looking around.

I carefully look around the wall when I see him carrying a woman's limp body; a tanned blonde wearing a tight purple dress. I see WV carved into her chest and several stab wounds. He heartlessly tosses her body into the hole. When I see his short beard and cleft chin, I know it's him. Chuck Archer. Now I know where he hides all the bodies. Maybe the bodies from the previous cases are still here and we can finally put an end to the WV murderer.

He begins to carry another body over. This is making me sick. I close my eyes, "Linda wake up, wake up now."

My body twitches as I awaken from the dream. It's crazy that I can control my dreams to the point of waking myself up. I guess that's a good thing. Its 5:30am, close enough to my alarm. There's no way I'll get any more sleep. Luke is still passed out.

I go to check on Michael and he's sound asleep as well, so I head downstairs to put on some coffee and give Fredrick a call. If we can find Chuck's hidey hole soon, then we can put him away forever and save of the lives of many innocent women.

"Hello," Fredrick answers in his calm and collected tone, even early in the morning.

"Hey, sorry if I woke you."

"I don't sleep much anyway. What's up?"

"I think I have a lead on Chuck Archer. I had a dream and found his burial site. It's a long stretch because I don't have specific details, but with the whole department helping, I think we can find it."

"Oh, that's great news, please explain everything. I'm taking notes as we speak." I tell him about the private beach with the rock maze.

"Hmm, there are so many different beaches in this area. Shit, this is going to be tough, but we better get started now. We have a lot of ground to cover. I'm going to get my whole department and the fire department onto this search. Thank you so much, Linda. I'll keep you posted."

"Thanks and good luck."

I sit at the kitchen table in silence thinking about the bodies, the ship, and Tom. I'm going to drive myself crazy if I don't do something. I decide to cook a nice breakfast for Luke and I.

As I'm scrambling the eggs flashes of Chuck throwing the bodies into the ground pound in my head. I drop the spatula onto the floor and hold myself up by the counter as I stumble. I cry out in pain. BAM! Another shock into my head. I'm weak and vulnerable right now as I cradle myself on the floor. Tom's voice spins in my head.

"Fight it Linda, control it, and think of darkness. Deep breaths, control, control." I keep repeating these things to myself over and over.

I calm down when Luke runs over to me and grabs me in his arms. "I'm ok, I'm ok. I was able to control it."

Luke looks at the spatula on the floor along with the spilled eggs. "It doesn't look like you controlled it in time."

"It hit me like a ton of bricks and came out of nowhere."

"Did you have another dream about Tom?"

"No, it was about Chuck. I found out some information. I've already called Fredrick and he's on it."

He picks me up and carries me over to the chair without saying much. He finishes making the breakfast. I know he's just as frustrated as I am. I carefully get up to get Michael as I hear him crying.

We all sit around the table and finish our breakfast and coffee. "Are you excited about your first day back at work?"

"Yes, beyond excited. It'll be good for me to stay busy and keep my mind off things."

"Are you going to be ok today?"

"Yes, Luke. I'll be ok, I promise. Like I said, I'm getting better at controlling the flashes. Soon enough I should be able to stop them completely."

"I hope you're right."

I walk into the shop as Sarah and Bobby are setting out all the pastries. I stop as I walk in and take a moment to look around. Gosh, I've missed this place; the colorful walls, floor to ceiling windows, and the smell of coffee. It has been way too long.

"Linda! Aren't you a sight for sore eyes! Get over here and give me a big hug," Sarah says as she prances over smiling.

Bobby follows closely behind. "We're so glad to have you back. It's not the same without you," Bobby says as his gigantic arm muscles wrap around me for a hug.

"Thank you both. I'm so happy to be here." I feel like a little kid in an amusement park. I'm so happy.

The day is going great! Many regular customers have told me how much they've missed me and talk about Michael. This is the first time I've been back to work since the coma and it's a little strange at first. I think about the times Tyler came in and how many times Tom was in here.

I have to stop dwelling on the past and enjoy the moment. I can't let people ruin my coffee shop. This shop is my life.

I receive a few texts from Luke throughout the day checking on me. I couldn't be happier here back in my shop.

I go into the back room to feed Michael. I decide to take a lunch break for myself as well. I'm not as tired as I thought I'd be so I decide to put more hours in. I don't want to be alone and in my head right now. Hearing all the people's laughter and conversations is soothing.

Sarah comes back into the break room and sits with me. "So how has this place been without me? I haven't gotten a chance to sit down and talk to you in a while."

A concerned look flashes upon her face. "Well it has been a lot of work but it has been good." She looks away from my glance. There's something she isn't telling me.

"What is it, Sarah? You've been my best friend for a long time and I know when you're hiding something."

"I don't want to put any more stress on you or make you worry."

"Too late, I'm already worried, so spill it."

"Tyler has stopped by a few times since you've been gone. He asks how you are and when you'll be back to work."

My heart drops into my stomach. "I thought he was in a

mental hospital or something?"

"He was in one for a few days to get tested. Remember the bipolar disorder?" I nod in agreement. "Well they just put him on meds and let him go. They couldn't find anything else wrong. Trust me, he told me all about it. He seems calmer and not the same Tyler as we knew."

"I don't care if he isn't the same Tyler. He's still coming in here wanting to see me."

"What he said to me was that he wants to make amends and apologize for everything."

"I've heard that one before."

"I really think he means it this time." I can't believe she's taking his side on this. Am I being too stubborn about this or too bitchy? I feel like I have the right to be. Sarah can tell I'm aggravated.

"I just wanted to give you a heads up in case he comes in while you're working, which I expect he will at some point."

"Thanks." I change the subject before I get too upset. "So how are things between you and Bobby?"

A huge girly grin appears on her smooth face, "Well..." she says as she holds up her hand for me to see her wedding ring.

"What? When did you get married and how come I didn't know?!"

"We decided to do it silently and on our own. We took a trip to Vegas to get married a few weeks ago."

Sarah and Bobby are definitely the type to get married in Vegas. They're both very outgoing.

"I wish you'd have told me. I could have gotten you a present at least."

"No, no girl. You had a lot going on. We didn't tell many people. We're very happy that we got married that way."

"Well then I'm happy for you. But the next good news you have you better tell me right away!"

"Yes ma'am, I promise I will." I give her a kiss on her cheek and a hug.

I lay Michael down for a nap. "Ready to get back to work?"

Sarah smiles. "You bet I am."

***

Luke gets off work early and picks me up. On the short ride home Fredrick calls me. "Hey, did you find his hide out?"

"Yes we did. Surprisingly he found a nice burial ground in a deserted area of Seabrook Island. Your dream was exactly right. It looked like a maze of big rocks."

"Oh, thank god. Will this be enough to put him away?"

"We're going to gather DNA off the bodies and take his DNA. Hopefully it's a match."

"It will be. We both know this is him."

"Yes, but this also means there's an innocent man in jail. I'm going to interrogate Chuck now and show him the pictures of all these bodies. Make him confess. He must have framed Wilfred Valentine. Using his initials on the body was a smart move."

"I know you'll figure it out. You're too good of a detective not to."

"Thanks Linda but don't get too ahead of yourself. Tell me that when Chuck is in jail. I'll keep you posted. Thank you again."

"Anytime. Goodbye."

"Well they found his burial site. Now they're putting the DNA together and hopefully getting a confession."

"That's great news. I'll keep my fingers crossed."

Over dinner we talk about some of Luke's surgeries for the day. I begin to think about what Sarah said earlier. Should I tell Luke about Tyler? I know he'll freak out, but I shouldn't hide something like this from him.

I let out a sigh," So, Sarah told me some things that have happened at the shop while I was gone."

"What happened?"

"Tyler has come in a few times asking for me."

A blank, cold, angry look forms on his face; a look I've seen way too many times recently. "What the fuck? And she didn't tell him to leave it alone?"

"I guess not. She told me the medicine has changed Tyler completely and he isn't the same Tyler we used to know."

"That doesn't make the situation any better. He tried to hurt you, almost kill you. What is this, like de vu all over again? Tom and Tyler are at it again. I swear they're like a team or something." *A chill runs down my back. The two of them working together is a scary thought. No, it can't be. Or could it?*

"If I can't do anything about Tom right now then I'm doing something about Tyler. What's Fredrick's number?"

"He's busy at the station with Chuck."

"I don't care. Why are you so hesitant about this? Aren't you afraid of Tyler?" *Come to think of it, I don't know why I'm hesitant. I guess I feel bad, but for what? Tyler did try to kill me. Why would I want to see him again or be put in another situation? Luke is right, he has to do something about it.*

"Yes, I am."

"Then let me take care of it and protect you."

"Alright babe." I read Fredrick's number to Luke as he types it in his phone.

"I'm calling him now." Luke is pacing around on the phone outside on the patio. I clean up the dishes and wait impatiently to see what the boys are discussing and what plan they make up.

Luke walks back in and seems to have taken a 180 turn. He's calm and relaxed. "Well?"

He smiles. "Fredrick is going to take care of Tyler."

I look at him waiting for a more detailed answer. "Ok, what exactly does that mean?"

"He's going to pay him a little visit. Tell him to back off and if he steps foot into the shop again or anywhere close to you then he's going to put a restraining order on him."

I feel relief. "Ok good."

He kisses me softly on the lips. "I'll do anything in my power to make sure you're safe."

I kiss him again. "I know you will baby, and I can't thank you enough for that."

"Now put down those dishes and let me finish cleaning them."

"Yes sir," I say with a wink.

I jump up on the kitchen counter and watch him clean the dishes. What man takes this good of care of his woman? Even after being together for a while now, I still can't get used to this treatment.

He glances over at me as he closes the dishwasher. "What's that grin for?" he asks as a sexy grin starts to appear on his face.

"Just thinking how lucky I am."

He comes over and puts his body in between my legs. "Oh yeah? Well we both know who the real lucky one is." He kisses me hard entering his tongue into my mouth. Next thing I know our clothes are flying all over the kitchen. He carries me over to the kitchen table, and we have mind-blowing sex.

By the time we're done my body is tingling all over. We're both sweating and out of breath. He gently carries me upstairs to the bathroom. We end the night with a warm, comforting shower.

***

I'm riding on the passenger side of a helicopter. I look below me and all I see is the beautiful blue ocean. Where am I? "Ok, miss we're getting close to the coordinates you gave us."

Coordinates? What in the world is going on? Then it dawns on me. I bet this is where the cruise ship sunk! He's speaking into his headset. "We're approaching 17 degrees North, 72 degrees West."

"What are you going to do when we reach that point?"

"We're following a submarine. Once we both get to this point, they're going to search for the ship."

"Oh ok," I say as I nod my head. I'm still confused by this situation.

"So miss, if you don't mind me asking, how did you find this place?"

That's a good question. I don't even know the answer to this one. All that matters is that I'll know as soon as I wake up.

"It's a long story and I'd rather not go into detail."

"Ok. They're at the exact coordinates. They're searching the premises now."

My hands begin to sweat and nerves overwhelm me. I really hope they find this ship. I fiddle with my thumbs as we anxiously wait to hear back from them.

He holds his earpiece close to his ear as he concentrates on what they're saying. "You're never going to believe this. You were right. The cruise ship is at the bottom of the ocean."

I don't know what to feel right now. Relief? Pain? Sorrow? All those people, all those bodies at the bottom of the sea; what a horrible image.

He looks over at me with a questionable look. "How in the world did you know?"

I ignore his question and glace out at the ocean of death. I close my eyes and all I see is the dark, blue water.

Chapter 9

I wake up with tears in my eyes thinking about all the families waiting to hear news about their loved ones and all the innocent people who lost their lives. That ocean is a graveyard. I lie awake staring blankly at the ceiling. The coordinates 17 degrees North, 72 degrees West replay over and over in my head. Let's just hope my dream is right.

I glance over at my clock. It's 3:00am. I wish I can call Fredrick right now. Michael begins to cry over the baby monitor. It's like he knows when I wake up. Almost every night he begins to cry when I awake from a dream. We must have a strong connection.

I walk in his room and hold him tight as we sit in the rocking chair. I gaze down into his blue eyes. "I love you so much, but it'd be nice to get a full night's sleep without any interruption." He begins to feed. "But to wake up in the middle of the night to my beautiful baby makes it all worth it. You really are an easy baby to take care of. I've heard horror stories about how babies cry all the time, but not you, Michael. You're a true miracle."

I rock Michael and sing Beautiful Boy to put him back to sleep. "Before you go to sleep say a little prayer, Every day in every way, It's getting better and better, Beautiful, beautiful, beautiful, Beautiful boy."

I see Luke standing in the doorway smiling at me as I sing. I walk up and kiss him as I continue to rock Michael. I lay him back in his crib and give him a soft kiss on the forehead. "Sweet dreams, my beautiful baby boy."

Luke holds me in his arms as we both fall asleep. We wake up to my alarm. Luke rolls over and gives me a good morning kiss. "How was last night? Any dreams?"

"Yes, about the cruise ship. I know exactly where it sunk down to the exact degree."

"Wow, that's great."

"Now I hope the families can at least be at peace knowing exactly what happened and where they are."

"I hope so too."

I call Fredrick as Luke whips up some breakfast. "Any news on Chuck?"

"Yes, I'm glad you called. He wasn't giving us any information in the beginning. He was sloppy on a few of the murders because we found his DNA on some of the bodies; a complete match. He was going down for years with the information we had, even without a confession. Knowing that information he eventually confessed. He said Wilfred Valentine was the perfect person to frame because he was always known as a creep. He spent time doing research on Wilfred and following his every move. Thanks to you, Linda we just put away an active serial killer who has been killing for years and would have kept killing for many more years to come."

"You're welcome. I just helped with some small puzzle pieces – you and your detectives put the larger puzzle together."

"Did you have something else you needed to tell me?"

"Yes, I have some good news. I know exactly where that cruise ship sunk. I'll give you the coordinates."

"Holy shit, this day keeps getting better and it's only the beginning. But you know Linda, if these coordinates end up being a match, detectives, the FBI, cops, and reporters all over the U.S. are going to wonder how we found out that information. If we aren't careful, people might start to think that we're involved with cases."

"You really think people will consider that an entire police department could be in on these terrorist attacks and murders?"

"They'll start investigating our department, I can guarantee it. How else would they think we found out information that could only possibly be found by being there at the scene or being a part of the crime?"

"Fuck, I never thought about it that way. What do you suggest we do?"

"I think you need to tell the reporters about your gift."

My mouth drops open at the statement. "No fucking way. People will think I'm crazy. No one will believe me."

"They will if you tell your whole story. They will after the cruise ship news leaks."

"You really think so?"

"People are naïve. They'll believe it."

"I don't know. I need to think on it."

"Ok, while you do that I'm going to contact some people in D.C and contact the Navy to see if they can search the coordinates."

"Thank you, Fredrick."

"No, thank you. I'm sorry that you're stuck in a stressful situation, but honestly I think you'll feel better if you tell your story. You'll be an inspiration to many."

"I'll think about it."

"When you become famous, don't forget us little people here," he says with a small laugh. This is the first time I've seen a somewhat funny side to Fredrick. It's nice to know he isn't always serious.

I laugh at his statement. "Don't worry, I could never forget you all. Plus if this does happen, I'm not leaving Charleston and working for anyone else. They're just going to have to deal with it. I still want to live my normal life here with my coffee shop."

"Think about the business it'll bring to your shop. You'll have people all over the U.S. coming to visit."

"Yeah, maybe you're right. Talk to you later."

"I'll be in touch," Fredrick says as he hangs up. *People from all over the U.S? It might help my business, but so many people will know about me, about my shop, where I live, come to think of it. This may benefit my business, but it may make my nightmare of a life even worse.*

"You look deep in thought. Is everything ok?"

I explain to Luke what Tom said and what could happen if all this leaks. "Well if you decide to do this, it means I'm going to have to work even harder to protect you."

I smile at his comment. "I don't know how I feel about this."

"How about we just wait and see what happens after Fredrick talks to everyone."

"Ok, but we need to be prepared."

"And we will babe, so don't worry."

Luke drops me off at work. Now's the time to relax and do what I love the most.

***

The next couple of days go by fast. Nothing intense happened and I didn't have any dreams, flashes or shocks. Now how long will this peace last? Not very long, I suppose. I haven't heard from Fredrick yet. I'm assuming it might take a few days to find the coordinates. Tyler hasn't stopped by the shop all week. Luke told me yesterday that Fredrick went and had a word with him.

I lie in bed on this beautiful Saturday morning. The sun is pouring through our windows making our turquoise walls shine. Luke stretches and yawns. He rolls over on top of me and looks me in the eye. "Good morning beautiful."

I instantly smile. "Good morning baby."

"How about a full out breakfast packed full of eggs, sausage, turkey, whole wheat toast, fruit, all sitting on the porch with a nice cup of brewed coffee?"

"Mmm, that sounds perfect." Luke smiles and gets out of bed. He begins to put a shirt on.

"Woah woah, what do you think you're doing? You aren't putting a shirt over that sexy muscular body of yours."

Luke's smile takes up his whole face. "Alright fair enough, but that means you can't wear one either."

"No, no, I still have tons of baby fat I need to get rid of. It's been a while since the coma. I'm going to start working out today."

"Babe, you look beautiful just the way you are."

"You have to say that because you're my husband."

"No I don't. I mean it when I say it."

"Thanks babe, I just want the body back which I had before I was pregnant. I'm determined to do it! I'm going to start light today with a run. Then I'll have Mom watch Michael for a bit and go back to the gym this week."

"Ok, babe, just don't overdo it."

"Don't worry, I won't." We begin to eat our wonderful breakfast and discuss something fun to do for the day when my phone rings.

I've been anxiously waiting for Fredrick's call. "Good morning, Fredrick."

"Good morning, Linda. I hope I didn't wake you. I contacted many people and we're all going out to the coordinates you gave me today. I'm flying in the plane with some other detectives plus the news crew. The navy will be in charge of the submarine, and along with them came a search crew. It's going to take a few days to get out there and do the search. You probably won't hear from me until Monday or Tuesday. Keep your phone close and your fingers crossed. This could be a big story to break and our department will get a lot of recognition."

"That's great. I'll be praying. Did they ask you how you came about the coordinates?"

"Yes they did."

"And?"

"I told them from a close source and let it be. But if they do find this ship they're going to want answers. I won't tell them your name, but they will start investigating our department."

"Ok, thanks for not saying anything. I have a few days to make a decision."

"I support you either way. They won't find out anything suspicious at our station because we're all innocent so eventually they'll stop digging. It may take a while, but it won't last forever."

"Thank you, Fredrick." That makes me feel much better. I honestly don't want the entire US knowing about my talent. After I get off the phone, Luke, Michael, and I sit out on the patio. My parents unexpectedly walk up to the patio.

"Well good morning to this beautiful looking family," my Mom says as her curly hair blows in the wind. Not to mention her dangling dolphin earrings. She has the strangest taste in clothes and jewelry, but it definitely suits her.

Dad walks up in Adidas black shorts and a white and black tank top. He looks like his usual athletic self.

"Well good morning. This is a nice surprise," I say hugging them both.

"We have a surprise for everyone. We know you've been stressed lately. Well when are you not?" We all laugh. "Anyway, your Dad and I wanted to do something special for everyone, so we booked a Dolphin Eco-Tour for this afternoon!"

"Aw guys that's awesome! I've lived here my whole life and still haven't experienced that."

"Well now you will and we'll go as a whole family," smiles Mom.

"Do you think Michael will be ok?"

"Oh yeah, infants under two get in for free. Just keep him in your carrier and you should be fine. It'll be an hour and half long. If you get tired of holding Michael you know I'll be happy to help."

I get overly excited as if I'm a kid all over again. "This is great, I can't wait!"

"Thank you both for doing this," Luke says.

"It's our pleasure," Dad says with his kind smile.

The water seems to be pretty rough. The boat is swaying heavily and I begin to get a little motion sickness. I hand Michael to Mom. "Are you feeling ok?" Mom asks.

"No, I think I'm going to be sick." Luke walks me over to the side of the ship and places his hand on my back. I put my hands on the railing and look over at the water. You'd think the railings would be a little higher for safety reasons.

"You doing alright, babe?"

I nod in my head. "I'm alright."

All of a sudden flashes of Tom's voice echoes like a loud train through my head. "*I'll always be with you*" I hear over and over again. A sharp pain shoots though my head as if I've been hit with a ton of bricks.

I feel dizzy and my mind starts fading. Luke's voice becomes faint. My knees buckle. I grip the railing as tight as I can to brace my fall. I'm too weak to hold myself up. Complete darkness takes over.

I wake up to drops of water splashing on my face. I inhale air as I sit up quickly. "Shit, Linda you scared the crap out of us!" Mom says with tears in her eyes.

I hold my head. "This is the first time I've passed out since the time I fell down the stairs. I think it's because I'm vulnerable right now since I was feeling sick."

"We need to get you home asap," Luke says as he hands me a Gatorade.

I start to panic. "Michael? Where's Michael?"

"Shhh, don't' worry, he's with your Dad sitting on the bench inside."

"Phew, I'm glad he wasn't in my arms this time around. Jeez, I put my own baby at risk when I hold him. What kind of mother am I?"

Luke grabs me and pulls me close. "Don't even go there, Linda. We all know that you're a wonderful mother. Don't go thinking things like that."

Tears begin to fall. The thought of hurting my baby boy makes my body ache with fear. *What if I pass out while holding Michael and no one is around? What if I really harm my son?*

The boat docks, Luke helps me up, and we all walk to the car. "We need to get some food in you. You still look as pale as a ghost."

"I'm not sure I can stomach anything. I still feel real queasy."

"I don't care, you need to eat. I don't want you passing out again," Luke says with concern.

"Alright, then soup and toast sounds good."

"Then that's what I'll get you."

I'm so fed up with being weak. I feel helpless and I don't like the feeling of not being able to control myself. Is this ever going to get better?

Night seems to fall quickly and sleep is calling my name. I close my eyes and wonder what I'm going to dream about tonight. Will I find out a new murder? Terrorist attack? Tom? There are so many options. How about a nice dream? I chuckle to myself. A nice dream? Yeah right. They're all nightmares in one way or another.

It's a beautiful clear night, I think to myself as I walk down Kings Street. The nightlife here is always busy. I sit on a bench and watch men and women walking around laughing, holding hands, having a good time. I watch girls stumble in their heels as they walk across the street. I chuckle and look around closely at what's going to come next.

I start to get up and walk around again when I'm taken aback by a big hand that grabs my mouth and face from behind. The man shoves my back into the bench. I can't see his face, and I have no idea if he has any weapon in his hand. I'm helpless. I try to kick and move but his other arm wraps around my chest.

"You're not going anywhere. You were supposed to be mine and I'm going to make that happen."

The cold, dark, raspy voice sends chills down my back. As soon as he speaks, I know this is Tom.

Tears begin to fall down my face but are caught by his hand still covering my mouth. I begin to breathe harder. My nose becomes stuffy from the tears making it hard for me to breathe. I start to panic heavily. I kick my feet hard on the ground and wave around, hoping someone will see me. Tons of people are walking around, so why can't

76

anyone see me?

"No one is going to help you, Linda. Think about it. I'm in jail right now. How can I be out in the streets wandering around?"

My mind becomes hazy and confused. How is he doing this? I stop moving and give up. "Yeah, not what you think, huh? The dreams seem so real, like your normal ones, don't they? Remember Linda, we were partners. I knew what your dreams were like and what they consist of. I'm in total control and you can't fight it. I'm getting closer to having you for good. You're going to be stuck with me FOREVER."

The word forever replays in my head. I begin to sob. His hand moves from my mouth and down to my throat. I take a breath in and out. He begins to squeeze my neck hard. I'm slapping his hand and kicking my feet trying to get him to stop.

"No way out, Linda. It's coming soon, the end of you; you'll be lost in a nightmare."

I begin to fade out as dark spots take over my vision. My chest feels heavy as I try to gag for air. My throat is getting tighter, my breathing is becoming shorter, and my vision darker.

Chapter 10

I wake up to my body trembling with fear, pain, and shock. I can't stop shaking. My entire body is in pain. I feel like I'm lying on a bed of sharp needles. "Luke, Luke." I cry out, tears pouring.

"Baby, what's wrong? What can I do?" Tears form in his eyes. The look of fear and worrying submerges his face.

"I can't move. My body is in too much pain."

"Do you want me to call someone? What can I do for you?"

I shake my head in disagreement. "Just lie here with me. It'll pass. I just need to rest."

"Ok, baby." Luke lies besides me gently rubbing my head.

The pain starts to fade. I concentrate on breathing and slowly moving my body parts. The thought of Tom rushes through my head and tears fall again. I shake my head from side to side. "It happened again, it was Tom. This time he actually showed up and laid his hands on me. He's able to control my dreams. He puts me in situations that make me think it's a normal dream. I was trying to call out for help and no one could see me. How is he doing this?"

Luke's face begins to turn red. "That's it. I'm stepping in right now. As soon as Fredrick gets back from working on the missing ship I'm talking to him to see what we can do."

"Ok. He told me he was getting closer to being his forever. I'll be stuck with him forever." His voice keeps echoing.

"No, you'll never be his. I don't know what the fuck he's doing or how the fuck he's doing it, but we're putting an end to it. I'll do whatever it takes to end this."

"Thank you, Luke. I'm so scared."

He wraps me in his arms. "I know you are baby. Don't worry, I'll protect you."

***

Monday morning rolls around quickly. I'm glad to be getting back to work after the dream this weekend. I spent way too much time thinking about what Tom said and how he's able to control my dreams like he did. I've got to be stronger. They're my dreams, it's my life, and no one should be able to control me like that. I need to gain confidence and power, and fight him. Luke wants to do everything he can to protect me, which I understand, but in reality there's nothing he can do. I have to be the one to do it. But how? I don't know but I'll sure as hell find a way.

It's a busy day at the shop and I'm fixing coffee left and right. I definitely enjoy staying on my feet. The lunch rush is just finishing and things are starting to calm down. I begin to clean tables when I see a rush of people walking towards the shop. There are cameras and microphones.

"Sarah come quick, check this out. What the hell is going on?"

She rushes over and glances out of the window at the mob coming closer to our shop. "Woah, there must be something happening outside. Let's wait and see where they go and then follow and be nosey!" she says with a cheesy grin.

I laugh in response. "Ok, sounds like a plan." We both watch with excitement. The mob slows down as it approaches our shop.

Sarah and I give each other a questioning look then fix our eyes back on the mob. They're now in front of our door. Some woman is speaking to the camera. "Why are they at our shop?" Sarah asks with concern.

"I don't kn.." I pause. "Shit, this can't be happening." I realize that they're probably here about me. I haven't heard from Fredrick yet, but he promised he wouldn't mention my name.

"What is it, Linda?"

"I think I know why they're here. Remember my cruise ship dream?"

"Oh fuck. How do you think they found out it was you?"

"I don't know and I don't want to find out. Prepare yourself for what's coming next."

"Should we leave out of the back door?"

As we look at the back door the reporters barge into the shop. "Sarah, go and watch Michael please. I'll take care of this."

"Ok, be careful."

"Mrs. Jackson, Linda Jackson." That's all I hear from about seven different people. Cameras are flashing, and questions are being asked at the same time. The flashes of the camera sets off the flashes from my dreams. *Shit, no stop Linda. Stop it now, don't let them see you like this. Focus, be strong, stay calm.*

My phone is vibrating in my pocket. My gut tells me that it's Fredrick. It's too late now. It's time to make a decision. They're bombarding me with questions. "Mrs. Jackson, we know it was you who found the ship in the ocean. We've been told that you're a psychic, is that true? How did you know the exact coordinates of the lost ship? Do you believe you have a gift? We've been told you work with the FBI on solving crimes because you can see them before they happen. Is that true?" All these questions are asked by different people all at once.

I shake my head to try and think of what I'm going to say. I hold up my hand to the reporters. "Alright, if you want answers you have to be quiet. I can't take all of the questions at once."

They all fall silent at the same time, like an orchestra. "Yes, it was me who found out about the lost ship. And yes, I work with the FBI on solving cases. I believe I do have a gift. I can see crimes before they happen in my dreams."

A bunch of gasps leave their mouths as they drop in shock. "So the rumors are true, Mrs. Jackson?" a tall lanky man asks.

I nod my head in agreement. "Yes they are. I dreamt about where the ship was buried in the ocean, and I've helped with many previous local murder cases in the Charleston area."

"Why have you kept it a secret for so long?" a red-headed woman asks.

"Why? Because the world would think I'm crazy. How could anyone possibly believe that a small town girl who owns a coffee shop is psychic and can see the future via her dreams? It sounds crazy to all of you, doesn't it?"

Sarah pops her head around the corner giving me the thumbs up. I nod back at her. The reporters are silent to my response. "Exactly, that's why I didn't share my secret with everyone. Plus it's my own personal life, and no one else needs to know. Now that everyone knows, that's beside the point. Since I'm on the air I'm going to say this. I ask everyone out there to please let me be. I don't want to be bombarded with phone calls and questions. I work for CPD and that is it. I won't participate in any outside cases out of state unless I have a dream before. Everyone is more than welcome to come to my shop as we're always welcoming new customers, but I won't talk about my gift or what cases I've worked in on the past."

The reporters are still and quiet. Someone clears their throat. "I think that's fair enough, Mrs. Jackson. Thank you for sharing your story."

And that's it. They all put their cameras and microphones down and I'm no longer on the air. Each reporter comes up to me to shake my hand, "Thank you for being a hero Mrs. Jackson," the red-headed reporter says. Then each reporter also says thank you.

After they all leave I sit down and try to process everything that just happened. A few customers in the shop can't take their eyes off me. "Ugh," I sigh. I guess I better get used to the looks because I have a feeling that's going to be happening for a while.

Sarah walks back over with Michael in her arms. "Are you ok? You did a great job. It was like you were a natural."

"That was the most stressful thing I've ever done. I just hope it doesn't get too crazy around here. I'm afraid of what the outcome is going to be after this airs." I take Michael from her hands. I can tell he's hungry and tired.

"Well, we'll all be here for you." She doesn't say much else and gets back to work. I check my phone, and notice five missed calls from Fredrick. I can't believe he told them it was me.

I go in the back of the café to feed Michael and brace myself before I make an unhappy phone call to Fredrick. As the phone begins to ring, I try to think of what I can say without sounding too rude.

"Oh Linda, thank god you called me back. I hope I caught you in time."

I interrupt him before he says anything else. "No, you didn't. I was harassed by a ton of reporters. You promised me you wouldn't bring my name into it unless I gave you permission."

"I know, I know, and I'm so sorry. It wasn't me. Someone from the station leaked your name. Believe me when I find out who it is, they'll instantly regret giving your name up."

"Why would someone do that?"

"Someone who's trying to be an ass."

"Obviously someone in the station doesn't care for me or else they wouldn't have done it."

"And as soon as I find out who it is, I'll take care of it. What did you say to the reporters?"

"Just watch the news at 6:00 tonight and that way you'll get the full story," I say with an irritated tone.

"I'll watch it. Again, I'm sorry this happened. But maybe it'll benefit you in some way. At least I hope it does. If you receive trouble from anyone, please don't hesitate to call me. I'll be sure to take care of the situation."

"Ok, thank you. And by the way you'll be getting a phone call or visit from Luke soon. I'll let him explain."

"Uh, ok," he says with an inquiring tone.

Luke comes to pick me up. I start the closing down process. "No Linda, Sarah and I will take care of it. You've had enough to deal with today," Bobby says as he walks out the back room. He has been so busy cooking food, I hadn't even noticed him here today.

"Thank you, Bobby."

Sarah shouts over as she sweeps the floor. "Call us if you need anything."

"Thanks girl, see you tomorrow!"

I put Michael in my carrier and Luke grabs my hand as we walk out the door. "So what happened today?"

I shake my head. "Are you ready for this one?"

We sit down for dinner and discuss the situation; what happened, and what steps we'll take if certain things begin happening.

"I mean, we have to realize that this can cause fans, and within fans there are always obsessed crazy fans. I mean I've already dealt with that and currently still am. God knows I can't deal with another one. Then there's the situation where nothing may come of this, but I don't think I can get that lucky." I stop in mid conversation. "We need to turn on the news. I want to see how bad this turned out, and prepare myself for what's coming next."

Luke nods in agreement and we head into the living room. I decide to text May and my parents to turn on the news straight away.

I pop up on the TV. I quickly change to the other news station and there I am again. In fact, I'm on every news station in

Charleston. "Lovely, here goes nothing," I say as I sigh. Flashing at the bottom reads, "Talented young woman sees the future through her dreams."

"Linda Jackson admits that she was the one who found the coordinates to the missing cruise ship. She tells us her amazing and surreal story at her personally owned coffee shop right here in Charleston. We have a hero in our town, a true hometown hero. Take a listen here."

They air every single thing I said, including the part about leaving me alone. They flash the video on the inside and outside of my coffee shop. The reporter comes back on the screen. "As you can see, this magnificent and magical woman is our hometown hero. I think it's safe to say from all of us, thank you Linda."

Luke rubs my back. "You know, you sounded like a natural. Maybe you're cut out for the big TV business," he says with a wink.

"Ha, yeah right."

"I thought you did great. I'm proud of you, baby. This is definitely going to bring customers to your store and nonstop phone calls." As soon as Luke finishes that statement my cell rings.

"Don't worry, it's just Dad."

I talk to Mom and Dad for a while and as I do so May calls on the other line.

"Hold on, May is calling. I'll call you guys back later. Thanks for the encouraging words."

As soon as I switch calls May's screeching voice makes me pull my ear away from the phone. She thinks I'm the coolest sister alive and is happy that I shared my story. Her and my parents think I'll be an inspiration to many and they all believe I'm a hero. I have a hard time looking at it that way because of the pain and fear I experience every day. Maybe if I start looking at the positives of this gift, the pain and fear might fade away. It's a stretch but it might work.

As soon as I hang up the phone it rings again. This time it's Fredrick. "Well, you sure got your point across. I thought the story was very well done. I'm proud to be working with you."

"Thank you, Fredrick. I just hope my life isn't too hectic after this."

"You have lots of support and help here. You'll be fine,

I promise."

"Thank you." I hear scuffles in the background.

"Geeze, ok give me a second," Fredrick says with an annoyed tone. "My so called other half wants to say something to you. He looks like a little kid right now begging to talk to you."

I laugh at the thought of Arnold begging and jumping around. I can just picture it now. "Ok, put him on."

"Dude Linda, you're freaking amazingggg. I'm proud of you, you superstar."

"Thanks Arnold," I say laughing.

"Ok, I'll give you back to the boss man. I just wanted to tell you that."

I hear more scuffles. "Ok sorry about that."

"It's not a problem."

"Well, I don't want to keep you. Call me if you need anything."

Luke takes my phone. "Ok, it's time to turn this off for the rest of the evening. I don't want you stressing."

"Good idea!"

"I'm going in tomorrow to talk to Fredrick about Tom. I know the two of us can settle this."

"Ok, babe. Let's hope I can make it through the night without any dreams with him. If at any point you see me struggling in my sleep, wake me up. I'm afraid if he can control the dream as much as he did, that I may not wake up."

"Oh, please don't tell me that. I won't be able to sleep all night. Actually I may stay awake and keep an eye on you."

"No, don't do that. You need your sleep too."

"We'll see."

We both put Michael to bed and set our alarm clock for the morning. Luke kisses me softly. "Please, no bad dreams tonight. I'll pray for you."

I kiss him back. "Thank you baby, I hope it works."

I close my eyes and begin to drift away.

It's dark as can be outside as I walk towards what looks like a deserted old tunnel. I stop and stare at the gigantic haunting entrance to this tunnel. What do I do? Do I walk inside like an idiot or do I wait out here to see what I can find? I take a slow spin as I check out my surroundings. The eerie moon peers through the brushes of the trees, lighting up this tunnel in a chilling way.

I quickly turn around when I think I hear a ruffle from the trees. Fuck, I want to get out of this situation. My gut is telling me to stay because something is going to happen. My mind is telling me to get the hell out. I stand there frozen unsure of what to do. I hear an owl in the distance. I'm stuck in a horror movie situation right now. I honestly don't know if a creature or a killer is going to emerge from those trees. I make myself laugh as I picture a big foot slamming out from the trees.

I have to try and find some sort of humor in all this. Fear instantly takes over when I hear more ruffling, this time getting closer. I hear a struggle and some static mumbles. It doesn't sound like anything is coming from the tunnel. I need to hide myself and fast. I glance around and find a big tree right next to the opening of the tunnel. I quickly park myself behind the tree peeking out to see what's coming.

"Stop, it please, let me go," I hear an innocent voice say from the trees.

"Stop squirming you bitch and maybe it wouldn't hurt so much," says a deep voice. My heart starts to race as they get closer. The moonlight gleams onto the gravel leading into the tunnel, just enough light for me to get a good look.

Just then I see a man's back. He's dragging a woman by hair and the back of her neck. "Don't worry, we're almost there. Your life is about to end. Aren't you scared? And lucky for me I get the wonderful price of two!"

My stomach becomes nauseated. I hope he isn't talking about what I think he is. Either she has a child in her arms or a baby in her stomach. Please don't let it be that.

"Oh God no, please don't hurt my baby!" screams the woman.

Tears begin to flood my eyes. I can't stand to watch this. He drags her into the tunnel and I can see them passing me. The woman is dragging her heels into the ground. Just then I see her round belly. She's very much pregnant, not far from her due date.

Fuck, I can't let this happen. I quickly look on the ground for a weapon. I have to find something; I can't let this go on.

"Don't worry, I promise it'll be quick. You won't feel a thing." She screams out, "Bloody murderer."

"No need to scream, baby girl. There's no one around to hear you."

I pick up a sharp rock; it's the best thing I can find in this moonlight. I step out from behind the tree. "That's where you're wrong," I say to the man.

"What the fuck? And who the fuck do you think you are?" He drops the woman to the ground and she pants. She's still crying out.

He walks towards me. The glare of the moonlight shows his dark, bald head. I notice he's wearing sunglasses. "And you think your scrawny little ass can stop me?" he says pulling out a knife.

"I sure as hell am going to try." I don't know where this wonder woman is coming from, but I gained strength as soon as I thought about that man hurting the woman and her unborn child.

"Well how about you come and try, bitch?"

I look behind him and the woman is crawling away. I hope she can at least hide. I walk towards the guy with my sharp rock. I don't know how this is going to end, but at least the woman is safe for now.

He laughs as he walks towards me with his knife pointing upwards. We walk closer to each other and the fear of the unknown takes over.

Chapter 11

I wake up in distress when I hear Michael crying. I swear Michael's timing is always perfect. It's almost like he can sense my fear.

I sit with him in the rocking chair. "Thank you baby boy for being my savior." Luke walks in as I'm feeding Michael.

"Is everything ok, baby?"

"Yeah, Michael woke me up from my dream just in time."

His look becomes cold. "Tom?"

"Nope, a regular dream that I can tell Fredrick about." I let out a quiet laugh. "A regular dream? Funny how my murder dreams are starting to become normal. I wonder what it'd be like to have a normal dream."

"I know babe, but you're a hero."

"True, and I guess that makes up for it. I'll call Fredrick first thing in the morning to tell him."

"What was the dream?" I tell him about it as I bounce around with Michael.

"Wow, you're becoming braver. Trying to save the woman in your dream is a noble thing to do."

"I know, I can't believe I did that either, but instinct took over at the thought of him murdering a pregnant woman. I don't know if I'd do that in real life."

"Oh Linda, knowing you, you would. You care about others too much. Why do you think I worry about you so much? I know you'd put your life in danger to save another. That's why you're a hero."

"I hope I can keep up my image. What if I make a mistake? It'll be known everywhere."

"Everyone makes mistakes. Just keep going about your daily routine as usual and act like nothing ever happened. If you over-think this then it'll end up getting to you. Screw the reporters and all of that."

I nod in agreement. "You're right. I wonder what tomorrow will have in store for me."

"I only have on-schedule surgery tomorrow. It's a surprisingly light day. After I'm done I'm going down to talk to Fredrick. Then I'll come by your shop and keep an eye out. I have a feeling it might be packed and I want to be there in case something happens. The hospital will call me if there's an emergency."

"Ok, thank you babe."

I lay Michael back down. "Let's head back to bed. Only a few more hours of sleep," Luke says with a whisper.

My alarm goes off quickly. I want to go back to bed and sleep for hours. Luke rolls over and kisses me on the lips. "Good morning, beautiful. I'll go and put on some breakfast."

I can't help but smile. "Morning baby, and thank you."

I pick up Michael and head downstairs to call Fredrick. I tell him the day and place it happens. He's going to search for tunnels around the area and have men on them starting at dusk.

"Fredrick is going to be hanging around downtown today as well. He wants to keep watch on the shop in case something happens. After today he's going to have a cop on watch during store hours until this dies down a little."

"That's a great idea. I'm really starting to like Fredrick. He's great at his job."

"Yeah, he is. He cares a lot about protecting this town."

"Agreed. My surgery is at 8:00am. As soon as that's done I'll call him to see where he's at. Keep your phone on you at all times. I'll be checking in until I get there."

"Ok babe," I say as I stuff my face with a nice hot spoonful of oatmeal. The cinnamon flavor and the warmth of it tastes so good.

As Luke drives us to my shop I see a swarm of people from a distance. "Fuck, this doesn't look good."

As we get closer I see that there are no cameras or equipment, but a line of people all the way down Kings Street. "Holy shit. Talk about a booming business right now. I've never seen my store like this. This is awesome," I say cheerfully. My phone is ringing and I see it's Bobby. "Holy shit, are you seeing this?" I ask him.

"Yeah, Sarah and I are already inside getting everything ready.

We're going to be making a lot of coffee and I'll be doing a lot of baking. Know anyone that can come down and help for the day?"

"Umm, I can call my Mom and May. They'd be willing to help."

"Ok, that would be great. Come inside and call them, and then we'll open and get started. I'd keep the thought in the back of your mind of hiring another person."

"Oh, that thought is already in there. See you in a few."

I put the phone in my purse and look at Luke. "Alright, here goes nothing."

"I'm walking you in. I don't want them swarming you or getting too close, especially with Michael in your arms." I smile and nod.

We get out of the car and I hear yells from the line of people. "Linda, Linda over here. You're our hero. Thank you. God bless you." There are so many different comments coming from various directions. I could never get used to this attention. It's all way too weird for me.

"Thank you everyone for coming here. I appreciate the business! I hope you all enjoy the coffee and food. Bear with us as we only have three people working today. Some orders may take longer than others. Thank you again and we'll be opening in about five minutes."

They all cheer in response. Luke guides me through the crowd and opens the door.

I walk in with excitement. "Holy shit, this is so awesome!" I say to Sarah and Bobby who are hard at work.

"I know! Making that money today!" Sarah says with a high pitched, enthusiastic voice.

"All the pastries that I baked last night are out. I'm going to make more now and probably keep them coming all day," Bobby says.

"Thanks Bobby. It's going to be a hell of a day! Let me call Mom and May real quick."

Luke puts his hands on my arms. "Are you going to be ok?"

"Yes, I promise babe. Get to that surgery before you're late."

"Ok, I'll be back as soon as I can," he says kissing me on the forehead.

I call Mom first then May. I yell over to Bobby as I open the cash register, "Mom can help, but May is busy at work."

"Ok, one more person will help a ton."

"Well, let's open up shop!" says Sarah like a little kid.

"Bring it on!" I say.

They storm in, but in a linear fashion. I see so many new faces, including older couples, young people, parents with their kids, and even a few dogs! I've never had this many back to back orders since the shop has been open. I feel like I'm on a high.

Every customer says thank you to me. A few even ask for an autograph. I'm beyond thankful right now. Everyone is so nice.

Mom comes in about thirty minutes later. The line is still outside the door and the inside of the shop is just as full. Many people are starting to make their way outside. "Mom, thank goodness! Can you take Michael for a little bit while I continue working?"

"Wow, it's crazy in here! Yes absolutely. Are you doing ok?"

"Way better than ok. I feel like I'm running tons of caffeine!"

"Be careful. If you need a break let me know."

The white chocolate caramel is a popular one today! One of my regular customers comes up next. "Hey Jen, how are you this morning?"

"Not as good as you, I see! This is wonderful for you! Great interview by the way. Thank you for everything you've done and will continue to do. You know, you should totally write a book about this. People would love to know what it's like to predict the future with their dreams."

"Hmm, you know that's a great idea. I may have to consider that. Would you like your usual?"

"Yes please." Jen looks around the store. "Damn, someone is in my spot! I don't know if I like all these newbies," she says with a joking tone.

"Maybe it'll be good to change it up this time."

"Yeah, I think I'll sit outside. It's a beautiful morning and the water is truly glistening today!"

Time seems to fly by. The customers are never ending. Bobby has already refilled the pastries twice. He's now getting everything ready for lunch. The reporters start rolling in. "Shit, I was hoping there wouldn't be any press here today," I say to Sarah.

"From what it looks like, they're interviewing people standing in line outside. Hopefully they won't come inside."

The reporters make their way in a few minutes later. "This is the outcome from the interview of Linda Jackson last night. People are raving about her personally owned coffee shop, Sweet n Spice, in the heart of downtown. Nothing but good things are coming from these customers and the line is backed all the way down Kings Street. Let's get a look at the hero herself!"

I look up and the camera is pointed towards me. I don't know what to do so I smile and get back to work. It's the red-headed woman again her with bright pink lipstick. "Mrs. Jackson, I know you're busy but would you like to say a word about the business today?"

"I just want to say thank you for everyone who came out and who's still standing in line. I appreciate the business and all the kind words."

"Thank you, Mrs. Jackson."

A few more hours pass and the reporters leave. Luke, Fredrick, and Arnold come strolling in. "Woah dude, look at this place!" Arnold says with a loud voice.

I glance up and immediately smile when I see Luke. His bright white smile is glowing. He mouths, "You ok?"

I nod my head up and down and wink back. The three of them take a seat and look at the crowd.

"Hey Mom, can you come here please?"

She cheerfully walks out from the back. I take Michael from her arms. "Can you take over for a little bit? I'm going over there to see how the boys are doing."

"Of course."

I take a seat next to Luke. "Wow, it feels good to sit. I've been on my feet non-stop since we opened."

"Any weird customers or anything out of the ordinary?" Luke asks.

"Nope, everyone has been so nice." I tell them about Jen who told me to write a book about it.

"Not a bad idea," Arnold says. "Think about how you'll become even more of a star!"

"Yeah, I don't know about that. It's weird enough as it is right now."

Fredrick changes the subject quickly. "Luke told me what's going on with Tom. We've come up with an idea. But we won't talk about it here. After work we will."

My heart races at the thought of what they're going to do. Will I really be rid of Tom forever? "Ok, you all can come over for dinner."

"Sounds great, thank you. I've got men in the tunnels for tonight."

"I'm going to get back to work now."

"Ok, we're going to stay for a while and see how things go. It's almost close to closing time anyway."

I nod and head back behind the counter. As it nears closing time the line begins to die down. Finally the line is just inside the shop. I ring up another customer and hear the bell ring as the door opens. The door has stayed open all day so hearing the bell is surprising. I glance up and immediately gasp with shock when I see Tyler walk in.

What the fuck does he think he's doing? Is he trying to cause problems? Sarah sees and gives me the ok to leave. She takes over the cash register.

I walk out from behind the counter when Luke sees Tyler. Luke instantly gets up out of his seat, which falls loudly to the floor. *Shit, Luke is going to flip.* I walk over there to try and stop Luke from making any sudden or loud movements. I don't want to cause a scene.

Fredrick puts his hand on Luke's arm causing him to stop in his tracks. I walk over and grab Luke's other arm. "Babe, relax. Fredrick will take care of this."

"I can't believe this fucking asshole would show his face here," he says but not loud enough for anyone to hear.

Fredrick stands up. "Luke, take it easy. I've got this under control."

"You better file for a restraining order after this," Luke says.

"Don't worry, I'll take care of it," Fredrick says as he walks towards Tyler to escort him out of the shop. As Tyler walks out the door he glances back at Luke and I and gives us a vindictive and threatening smile. I've never seen him smile like that. Ever.

Luke pushes forward with anger. "That fucking piece of shit!"

I stop him in his tracks and look into his angry eyes. "Fredrick has got it Luke, please relax. I don't want any more of a scene." I've never felt his body this tense before.

I kiss him and he starts to relax a little. "I swear Linda, if he shows up again after the restraining order, I'm not holding back

92

next time. He's a fucking freak who's playing some sick game."

I give him a hug. He brings me close and holds onto me tightly. I feel safe in his arms. I head back over to the counter to ring up the last few customers. Sarah turns the open sign to closed. As I'm taking cash out of the register I hear a whisper coming from behind me. "Linda, it's almost time. You'll soon be mine."

I quickly turn around in panic. Nothing is there. I shake my head trying to forget that just happened. *How is he doing that? I have to be imagining things. What the fuck is going on?* All these thoughts run through my head as my body shakes. Flashes of Tom holding me down on the bench bang through my head.

I cry out in pain and fear and fall to the ground. I lie there and everything is spinning. "Linda, you will be mine." I hear whispering and echoing. Things start to fade. I can see Luke above me, saying my name but I can't hear anything. He starts to become fuzzy. Darkness takes over.

Chapter 12

"Get her some water and a cold wash cloth quickly!" I hear Luke's voice as I fade. I barley feel the cold wash cloth. I start to come back to reality. I slowly open my eyes and see Luke right above me. He gently picks me up by my underarms and places me in his lap. "Baby, are you ok?"

I gently nod my head up and down. I can tell by the sounds in the shop that all the customers have left. "Oh no, please tell me there weren't a lot of people in here to witness what just happened."

"Only a few. Bobby escorted them all out. No one could tell what was going on. Some were nosey but we didn't let anyone catch a glimpse of you."

"Oh, thank god."

"You've had a really long day. Let's get you home."

Mom brings Michael to me and kisses me on the cheek. "Are you sure you're ok, honey?"

"Yes Mom, I promise. Just a stressful and long day. I couldn't control my outburst this time."

She shakes her head. "It doesn't sound like you're ok to me."

"I know, but it's something I have to deal with for the rest of my life. Eventually it'll become every minute."

"Ok honey, whatever you say. I love you."

"I love you too, Mom."

On the car ride home my mind wanders. "I hope we hear from Fredrick about what happened with Tyler."

"I'm sure he'll stop by or call, but honestly I don't think you need that right now. What you need is rest. What happened back at the shop? What were the flashes?"

I know he isn't going to like hearing this. "Tom whispered to me that I'll be his. It sounded like he was right behind me. It was so weird."

A deep sigh comes from Luke's mouth. "Don't worry, that'll soon be taken care of."

"What plan did you and Fredrick come up with?"

He parks the car and walks around to let me out without answering my question. "We'll both tell you together at a later time."

"Luke, I'm fine now. I want to know what's going on." He continues to walk towards our front door without answering.

He opens the door and lets me walk in first. "Like I said, you don't need the added stress right now."

He shuts the door and turns to face Michael and I. "Listen, I know you're protecting me and you want me to be safe and relaxed, but not telling me these important things is killing me. It's my dreams that you're dealing with. I have every right to know what's going on now. If you keep holding off telling me then I'll become more upset and stressed."

He puts his hands on my shoulders. "Alright, alright, you're right. I'm sorry. I just don't like seeing these blackouts."

"I know you don't, but it's something we'll both have to get used to."

"I don't think I ever will." He shakes his head. "Anyway, I'll call Fredrick to see if he and Arnold still want to come over for dinner so we can discuss things."

"Ok, thank you," I say as I walk over to our suede sectional couch to relax. I begin to feed Michael as he calls Fredrick.

I turn the TV on to our local news station. And what do you know, there's the film from today. It's amazing how quickly they can produce itand get it on TV. I turn down the volume so I don't hear what they say about my shop. I look at the never ending line standing down Kings Street. I still can't get a grip on what happened today. I wonder if the next few weeks will be like that.

Luke walks back in. I take a minute to admire the tight white shirt he has on. I can see his muscles bulging. Oh, what a sight! "Ok, they're coming over in about an hour. I'm going to put dinner on."

"Sounds great, thanks babe. After I'm done feeding Michael I may lie down for a few minutes."

"Good idea." He looks at the TV and sits next to me. "Your story is already on. Turn it up, I can't hear it."

"I don't want to hear it."

"Why not, it's all good things?"

"I'm sure it is. I'm just tired of hearing people call me a hero. I need a break from all the paparazzi."

"Alright babe." Luke takes Michael from my arms to burp him. "You relax now. I'll lie Michael down in his crib."

As I lie my head on my pillow, I become tired. My eyes are heavy. I try not to think about Tyler or Tom so I can get some rest. *Think of darkness and nothing else; big deep breaths.* Next thing I know I'm fading into sleep.

Luke shakes me to wake me up. "They should be here in about five minutes." I stretch and sit up.

"Wow, I feel much better. It's amazing what a quick power nap can do."

"Good, come and have a seat."

Fredrick and Arnold arrive shortly after. "Hey dudes!" Arnold shouts as he walks through the door.

Fredrick shakes his head and sighs. "How are you two doing?"

I smile. "Much better now."

Fredrick gives me a questioning look. "Better now? Did something else happen?"

"She had another blackout about Tom," Luke butts in quickly.

"I'm sorry Linda, but we have an idea. I don't know if it's going to work, but it's worth a try. First our DA is taking Tyler to court to file for a restraining order. That should be issued and taken care of soon. What I'm going to need from you is a statement. I want you to tell myself and another witness who's going to type up what you say, exactly everything Tyler has done to you in the last year. This way you won't have to make a court appearance unless the judge orders one."

"Ok, I can do that."

"I'll need you to come in tomorrow and do that. I know it's a lot for you but we want to get that restraining order approved as soon as we can."

"I agree. I'll come down first thing in the morning."

"Ok, good deal. Next part of business is Tom. I don't quite understand the whole dream and psychic aspect of all this. You know how I think. It was hard for me to believe your talents in the beginning until I got to work with you firsthand. Previous to that I never believed any of that stuff existed." Luke serves the chicken as we all talk.

I nod. "I understand. It took me a while myself."

"I had no idea that Tom has the same gift as you or how in the hell he's able to control communicating with you through your dreams, and I'm not even going to begin to think how it's happening, but it is and it needs to be stopped before something bad happens. Luke told me everything, but I want to hear every dream and what it consisted of with Tom."

I tell him how it started with the glance at the fountain, to having the dream of him speaking to me only. And now he can also touch me. I explain how he can control the setting of my dreams, and how he has threatened to make me his and keep me in a dream state.

"How would he be able to keep you in a dream state?"

I shake my head and raise my shoulders. "I don't know. I guess it'd be like another coma. He must be able to control his sleep to where he can remain in a coma state. His gift is obviously a lot stronger and more controlled than mine. That's my only explanation."

"I have a hard time wrapping my head around all this."

"You're telling me. It's a shitty feeling knowing someone has the power to control my dreams. I have to practice fighting it, but I don't know how."

"I can't give you tips on how to do that but I can tell you what I'm going to do. I have some guards on the inside at the jail that I'm close with. Now this goes against everything I believe in with my job and it could get me fired. I might not be allowed to work as a detective ever again."

I stop him before he continues. "No, you're not putting your career and life in jeopardy because of me."

"If something happens to you and I know that I could at least have tried something that might have avoided it, I'd never forgive myself."

"Fredrick, I'm one small person compared to the many lives you've saved and will continue saving for years. It isn't worth it."

"I'm not arguing with you on this. I'm going to do it."

"Alright, continue, but if I don't agree then you're not doing it."

"I can pay off a guard to kill Tom in jail." My jaw drops at the shock of what just came out of his mouth. *Tom dead? The feeling of excitement rushes through me. I'll never have to worry ever again. I'll have total control of my dreams and concentrate on being the hero everyone says I am.*

"You really think that's going to work?"

"I've already talked with the guard and he's willing to do it."

My stomach turns to knots. "Fredrick, I wouldn't be able to forgive myself if you lost your job because of this."

"No one will find out. The only people that know are the three of you and the guard. I'm close friends with the guard and can trust my life with him. He knows the jail system and the cameras to avoid, and how to turn them off for a few minutes to get the job done."

"If Tom really dies, I'll have my life back. Then I'll be able to focus on my dreams and really help you out."

"You already help me out."

"I know, but I'll be able to concentrate even more without always worrying about Tom and if it's his dream."

"I understand," Frederick says as he sips his water.

"When is the guard going to do it?"

"Tomorrow night."

"And you'll call me when it's done?"

"Absolutely."

Luke puts his hand on my thigh. "Everything will be taken care of. This will all be over soon."

Luke starts picking up everyone's dishes. Fredrick gets a phone call and steps outside. "Arnold, are you sure Fredrick knows what he's doing?" I ask.

I've never seen a serious look on Arnold's face like I do now. No smile, and his eyes are open and concentrated, "Yes, I've worked with Fredrick for many years. He's completely trustworthy and although he plays by the book, he can play the game well. He's a very smart man. He wouldn't do this if he didn't think he could get away with it. I promise you have nothing to worry about."

That makes me feel so much better. "Ok, good."

Fredrick walks back in. He has the perfect posture all the time. "Ok, my men are in place at a few different tunnels around the area. One of the tunnels is surrounded by trees and seems like the same description you gave us."

"Ok good. Hopefully I'm not wrong about this one."

"I'm sure you're not. I'll let you know what happens as usual. We're going to head out now. You get some rest and come down to the station tomorrow. You'll have a lot going on tomorrow."

"Yeah, I hate all the waiting around to hear information. As soon as I'm done at the station I'm going to work so I don't spend all day thinking and panicking."

"Good idea. Well guys, thank you for dinner. It was wonderful. Enjoy the rest of the evening," Fredrick says as he walks out the door.

"Yeah it was delish! Thanks," Arnold says with a cheesy grin.

Soon after they leave we're ready for bed. We shower and cuddle. Just as my eyes begin to close my phone rings. I don't recognize the number but decide to answer it anyway.

"Hello?"

"Hello, Mrs. Jackson. I'm very sorry to bother you so late. My name is Sargent Collins with the New York Police Department." My heart begins to race. *Fuck I knew I shouldn't have answered the phone. Can I just hang up now?* "I've been hearing many good things about you. The word is starting to travel around Police Departments." *It has only been two days! How in the world is the word traveling that fast?*

"If I may ask, how did you hear about me?"

"It was on the national news." My heart drops to my stomach.

"National news, already?"

"Yeah, they don't mess around with a great story like yours."

What did I get myself into? "Ok, may I ask why you're calling?"

"Well, I know you work in Charleston and that's the only place you want to work, which I completely understand, but we need some help on a series of kidnappings in the area. We've been having parents call in everyday saying their children have gone missing in the Pennsylvania Station, taken at the most crowded times of the day. We have no leads on any suspects. We're hanging dry and more children are being kidnapped every day. We could really use your help."

Fuck, how am I going to be able to say no to this? I promised myself I wouldn't get involved in any cases outside of Charleston, let alone another state. "What does this help consist of?"

The whole time Luke is sitting up in bed with a worried look.

"Well, we were hoping we can fly you out here and go over the case together. We'll put you up in a hotel and everything will be taken care of."

"I just had a newborn baby recently. There's no way my baby can travel that far."

"Ok, then do you have Skype on your computer?"

"Yes I do."

"Can we make a time to meet via that tomorrow?"

I pause for a few seconds to think this through. "Alright, I can do that, but I can't promise you anything. Sometimes my dreams don't work."

"Trust me, I'll take the odds. We're desperate for help."

"Ok, how about tomorrow at 11:00am?"

"That will be great. Thank you very much for your time and patience. I appreciate that you're willing to help us out."

"No problem. I'll talk to you tomorrow."

I hang up and look Luke in his eyes. "And so it begins. That was NYPD wanting my help. My interview was shown on national news."

"We knew this might happen. Be prepared for many phone calls."

"What am I going to do? You and I both know I'm going to have a hard time turning down cases that could save a person's life."

"I know you can't, babe. You're just going to have to go with your gut feeling. What's the case NYPD wants your help with?" I explain it to him. "Well, they're asking a lot from you. There isn't much detail."

"That's true, but their busiest time is usually the evening after work hours. I can start by putting myself there around that time. The only problem is how many people will be shuffling around. But the least I can do is try."

"I know you better than that. You won't try. You'll find information on this case and you won't stop until it's solved, just like every other one."

I sigh. "You're right, but I feel like I have no choice. I have to help. I want to be the hero."

"Then I'll be right by your side the whole time."

I kiss him softly. "Thank you. I better get some sleep. I have a long day ahead of me tomorrow."

He kisses me back. "I'll be here whenever you wake up."

I close my eyes and can't help but think of all the things that have happened today, what's going to happen tomorrow, and all the freaking information I have to wait to hear. Talk about a stressful life. My heart races as I think of everything. *Just don't think about Tom. Don't let him control my dreams. Don't let him win.*

***

I'm walking through a very crowded area. I hear lots of chatter and footsteps racing through the station. I look up in the big open space that this station fills thinking 'how in the hell am I going to be able to find any information out?' The kidnappings usually happen during the busiest time, so where should I put myself? Would this person kidnap a child near an arriving or departing train, or in the middle of the place? There are so many options and there's so little time.

I begin searching for children around the ages of the ones who have been kidnapped. The age ranges anywhere from 6-10. I look around and see many people but not as many small kids as I thought. As I'm watching the crowd I see a figure in the distance; a figure I know all too well wearing the same jeans and baseball cap as before. "Tom, what are you doing here?" I whisper to myself.

How the fuck is he doing this? This is my dream, how can he interfere? Then all of a sudden everything freezes. Every person in the station is still and I see Tom walking towards me. His eyes are hidden by his baseball cap but I can see that terrorizing smile forming as he gets closer.

"Leave me the fuck alone, Tom!" I yell out and hear myself echo.

"Oh Linda, haven't you learned yet? I'm in total control. And now you're a superstar. How is the world going to feel when you can't dream anymore? How are you going to stay a hero?"

"Why are you doing this? Why can't you just leave me alone?"

"Because you're supposed to be mine, so if it's in a dream state then so be it."

"How did you know about my interviews?"

"Linda, I'm a very well-known and high respected man in this community. I know a lot of people and I may have a few people on the outside keeping me posted. I know a lot more than you think."

Who would be contacting Tom about me? Someone close to me

again? When is this ever going to end? Ok, now is the time to try and fight this. Block him out, try to control my dream, gain the strength to fight him. I close my eyes and focus on darkness. Don't let him scare you.

"What are you trying to do? Fight me off?" He laughs. "You really think you can fight me off?"

Don't listen to him; just keep your eyes closed. I imagine Tom disappearing into thin air. Leave me be, Tom. I control my dreams and what happens. I can feel him fading. I don't open my eyes but I sense that he's slowly fading away. I whisper to myself out loud, "Just wake up Linda. Wake up and start over. You need to help find the kidnapper, don't waste your dream on someone so irrelevant to your life." I keep talking to myself hoping that I'll awaken from this nightmare.

I feel like I'm beginning to fade from this dream. I keep my eyes closed and count down the time until I open my eyes in my bed. I take deep breaths. Just when I think I'm starting to completely fade away he grabs me from behind, covers my mouth, and brings me down to the ground. He has a tight hold on me as his legs are wrapped around my body.

I feel the touch of his lip softly press against my ear as he whispers, "You can't get rid of me. Don't try to fight it, Linda. It'll hurt that much more if you fight me."

I'm speechless and tears form in my eyes. I lie there trapped, lifeless, and clueless.

Chapter 13

I wake up with a struggle as if I'm trying to fight free from Tom's arms.

"Get off me!" I say as I open my eyes and realize Luke is holding me. He lets go quickly. "Oh baby, I'm so sorry, I didn't mean for you to let go. It felt like I was still stuck in my dream."

"Someone was hurting you in your dream again?" I nod my head. "Tom?"

"Yeah. This time he interfered with my dream. I was at the train station trying to find out information and there he was. He made everyone freeze and it was just me and him. I tried to fight him off but couldn't. He was in total control once again."

He shakes his head and sighs. "Well everything will change after tonight. He'll never be a problem for you again, Linda." Deep down inside, my gut is telling me otherwise. I have a bad feeling that this isn't going to end for a while.

"I don't know, Luke. I don't have a good feeling about all of this."

"Fredrick made you a promise. I don't think he's going to break it."

"I'm not worried about Fredrick keeping his promise."

"Then what are you worried about?"

"Tom somehow finding a way to stop it."

"He's not that powerful."

"Luke, he's more powerful than you think."

"Obviously not powerful enough, if he's in jail."

"Unless he did that on purpose? Everything he used to do was for a rhyme or reason. Why not throw us off by being in jail? He told me in the dream he has someone on the outside helping him, feeding him information about me."

"What the fuck? Who would do that?"

"I don't know, maybe someone in the station? They all loved

103

Tom. What if he still has influence on some of them?"

"Well then we need to let Fredrick know so he can keep an eye out for the cops and detectives in the station."

"Ok," I say with a sigh as I glance at the clock that shows 3:34am. "I still have some time to try and find answers about the train station."

"Maybe you should wait to do that until Tom is dead. What if he comes to you again?"

"No matter what I dream, he can make his appearance. It's either I don't sleep, or I sleep and dream and take the chances of seeing Tom. I can't let him scare me away from my gift. That's when he truly wins."

"Alright babe. Like usual I'll be here when you wake up. If I see you struggling like I did just now, I'll do my best to try and wake you up."

"Thank you baby." Just as I'm about to close my eyes, Michael begins to cry. I get up and take care of my pride and joy and head back into bed with heavy eyes.

I'm back at the train station. This time everyone is moving and there's no sign of Tom. Ok, time to take care of business. I focus on the people and the children. Does anyone seem suspicious or out of the ordinary? Are there any children not holding onto their parents' hand?

As I'm searching I see a little girl who looks scared. She's crying and looking around frantically. She must have lost her parents. I need to get to her fast before someone else does. I can see the little girl in a pretty green dress from a distance. I see a man walking towards her from behind; a man with the look of vengeance on his face. His long blonde ponytail and a very smooth face obviously show no relation between the two. This man can't be her father or related in anyway. He has to be the kidnapper.

He walks closer to the girl as a smile forms on his face. I try to pick up my pace without causing a disruption. He puts his hands out to grab her, but I come in and quickly pick her up. I stare into the eerie blue eyes of the kidnapper. He doesn't say anything and gives me a cold and angry look. He can't do anything now. He doesn't want to cause any distraction. This is the first time he has failed.

The little girl looks at me, "Wh—who are you? Where's my mommy? I can't find her," she says as she begins to cry again.

I look up and the man is gone. "It's ok sweetie, I'll help you find her. My name is Linda Jackson."

"Will you help me find her?"

"Yes I will," I say with a smile.

I take her to guest services so they can make an announcement in the station about the girl. About fifteen minutes later I see a pretty dark haired woman running towards us. The little girl runs with arms open wide, "Mommy!"

The mother catches the little girl in her arms and sobs. "I'm so sorry, sweetie. I love you so much," and she smothers her with kisses.

"This woman helped me find you."

She looks up at me and I smile at her. She walks towards me holding onto her daughter tightly,. "Thank you so much for helping my baby."

"You're more than welcome."

"How can I repay you?"

"Don't worry about it, please. I'm just glad everyone is ok."

"God bless you." They walk away, her mom not letting her go.

I have a suspect, now I just need the date and time. I glance at my watch. It's Wednesday at 6:00pm. I have succeeded and now I can relax. I take a seat as I watch people hurrying by. I feel myself begin to wake up. I look up and see the man with the ponytail staring at me from the distance. His look gives me chills down my back. I stare back at him and smile.

I wake up a few minutes before my alarm goes off. I have a satisfying feeling that I finally found out some good information and will be able to help Sargent Collins and the NYPD without interference from Tom.

The alarm goes off and Luke instantly rolls over to me. "Did you find anything out?"

"Yup, I know who the kidnapper is, and when he's going to attack next." I go into more detail about the dream as I send a text to Fredrick.

Fredrick doesn't bother texting back. Instead, he calls right away. "Hey, just wanted to let you know that my men caught the killer from the tunnel. He surprisingly choked under pressure and admitted to his crimes. He targeted pregnant woman. He's a sicko. But another one in the books thanks to you."

"Don't worry about it." I begin to tell him about Sargent Collins and the NYPD. He doesn't sound too excited over the phone.

"So you are going to help them?"

"Yes, I already had the dream. I don't have to go there or anything. I'm skyping with him this morning."

"Well that's good. I hope you don't' get too many phone calls. I like having you as a partner."

"Don't worry. I'll never leave Charleston. If I can work on cases from home to help out others than I will, but I'm not going anywhere."

"Good, good. When are you coming down to the station to make your statement?"

"I'll eat some breakfast real quick then head over."
"Ok, it shouldn't take long. See you soon."

Luke takes me to the station and I run what I'm going to say about Tyler through my head. Fredrick already told me that I might have to go into detail about how it was when we were dating. I'm dreading that because not only is it going to make me feel uncomfortable but it'll be uncomfortable for Luke as well.

We get there and Fredrick and the AD are sitting there with a laptop ready to go. "Good morning Linda, sorry you had to come down here."

"It's not a problem. Anything I can do to help keep Tyler away from me."

"Ok, I'm going to start with some questions about your dating experience with Tyler. Then you can tell me what he has done to you since you've been broken up," says AD Stevens.

I nod. "Alright, I'm ready." I look over at Luke and his unhappy face.

"When did you and Tyler first start dating? How long did you date? Why did you break up? Did he keep contacting you after the breakup?" These are all questions that were hard to answer but I answered them in great detail.

Luke places his soft strong hand on my thigh for reassurance. I explain how many times he has come into my work and tried to hurt me. "He won't leave me alone and I don't know why." I look around the station as I'm speaking. *Who in here is leaking information to Tom?* I think to myself. I see a few policemen looking over here, but there are so many I wouldn't know where to begin.

"Alright, thank you for your time and patience. We definitely have enough information to get a restraining order."

106

"His lawyer will bring up the fact that he's bipolar and try to use that against us," I say.

Stevens shakes his head. "He just came back to you as he was on his medication. They'll use that excuse but he has still bothered you after therapy and medication. That won't work in court, I promise."

"Ok, I hope so."

"I'll give Fredrick the verdict once we know."

"Thank you for your help," I say as we get up and shake hands.

"No problem."

"Fredrick, I need to discuss something with you in private," I say. I look around the crowded room.

He nods his head and waves his hand to follow him. He shuts the door behind us as we walk into his office. "What's going on?"

"It's Tom again. He came to me in my dream last night. He told me there's someone leaking him information about me. He's being kept updated on everything that has been happening to me."

"Shit, think it's someone in the station?"

"I mean, that's the only explanation. Think about it; someone leaked my name to the news. Whoever that person is might be the one working with Tom."

"I didn't even think about that. Ok, I'll have to keep a close eye out. I may interview each person that works here and find what their affiliation with Tom was."

"Do you think that will really work? Tom was a good liar so I'm assuming the person working with him is a good liar, too."

"You're right. Well after tonight that may not be an issue. Maybe I can get my guard friend to threaten some information out of Tom so we get a name."

"It won't work. If Tom knows he's going to die, he wouldn't dare give out any information."

"You might be right, but it won't hurt to try."

"Alright." I glance down at my watch and realize it's getting close to 11:00am. "I need to head back and get ready for the skype call with Sargent Collins."

"Ok, thanks for your time again. Don't worry about Tom. It'll be over soon enough." *Yeah that's what you think. I know it won't be over.*

I nod and smile as we walk away. "God, I'll be so glad when Tom is dead and gone," Luke says as he drives off. I sit there in silence. Something deep inside me is telling me that it won't be as easy as everyone says.

Luke grabs my hand. "Are you ok?"

"Ye-yeah. I'm just thinking about this skype call, trying to gather all of my facts so I'm ready."

As soon as we walk into the house, I put Michael in his crib and set up the computer then sit in front of it. I feel a little nervous, but I'm not sure why. Maybe it's because I'm about to become involved with a case in an area I know nothing about. As I think more about that, the more nervous I become.

Just relax, be confident, and show that confidence to the Sargent. You're a hero, don't forget that. I keep telling myself.

I prop up in the chair as I receive the incoming call. I nervously click 'accept call.' A tanned, sandy blonde-haired and blue-eyed man is on the other end. For some reason he's not what I would have pictured him to look like after hearing his deep voice over the phone. "Good afternoon, Mrs. Jackson. Thank you so much for taking the time to help us out over here at the NYPD."

"Hello, Sargent Collins, and you're more than welcome. I'm glad to help. Before we go into detail, I had a dream last night about the kidnappings."

His eyebrows rise in surprise, "Oh really? It happens that fast?"

"It all depends. My dreams can vary."

"This is great because we had no suspects or even any idea of what the man or woman looks like."

I smile. "I can tell you exactly what he looks like."

"Thank God! Give me a second and I'll get our sketch artist." He makes a quick phone call. I become more relaxed and comfortable as the conversation goes on.

"Ok, Mrs. Jackson he'll be here shortly."

"Ok, and please call me Linda."

He nods his head. "Linda, tell me what happened in the dream. Do you know his next attack?"

"Yes I do," I smile and say with confidence. He's nodding his head as I speak, and writing down information.

"Wow, I can't believe this. I mean, I've heard you have this gift but to be able to work with you and hear the dreams is pretty impressive. Charleston Police Department is very lucky to have you on their side."

"Thank you. I appreciate the kind words, but you can really thank me after this guy is caught and my dream was correct."

"I'll do that then." He looks up from the camera. "Oh, here's the sketch artist now. I'll have you describe the man, woman, and child and then we'll be finished."

After about ten minutes of giving descriptions the conversation is over. "Thanks again for your time and help."

"You're welcome. I hope it helps."

"Have a nice day, Mrs. Jackson."

"Goodbye Sargent Collins." I click the end call button and take a deep breath.

Luke peeks his head into the computer room. "Well, how did it go?"

"It went really well and I'm glad I did it!"

"Good babe, I'm glad. Come and eat some lunch. I whipped up something quick and yummy."

***

Night falls quickly and I begin to grow anxious thinking about what the guard is going to do Tom. "I wonder how the guard is going to kill him?" I speak my thoughts out loud as we lie in the dark ready for bed.

"Don't think about it, either way it'll be done." We lie there in silence. I don't know if I'll be able to get any sleep tonight. Luke rolls over and kisses me on the lips. "Try to get some rest and when we wake up tomorrow, it'll be a new day."

"I'll try," I say as I give him another kiss.

He falls asleep quickly, but I continue to lie there with my eyes wide open. I softly get out of bed and go into Michael's room. Surprisingly he's awake but not shedding a tear. He's gazing into space. "Hi baby boy. What are you doing awake?" I say as I gently pick up him out of his crib.

He gives me a precious smile. I rock him in the rocking chair as I sing him a lullaby. I glance down and his eyes are closed. I continue to rock and hum. My eyes become heavy.

I feel the soft, cool sand beneath my feet as I slowly walk along the beach. The ocean looks mesmerizing with the reflection of the moon shining brightly. I take a moment and smell the salty breeze flowing in the wind and gaze into the deep, dark, mysterious ocean. I feel a gentle caress through my hair, and a hand taking mine. I turn to my right and my wonderful husband is standing with me. Finally a good dream? At least I hope so.

We don't speak to each other. We stand there hand in hand glancing out to the ocean. I turn to face him, wrap my arms around his neck, and kiss him. Our tongues meet each other's and start moving in sync. He then gently kisses my neck and brings his lips to my ears. "You can't stop me, Linda. That was a good try, but the guard didn't stand a chance. You'll never get rid of me." Tears form in my eyes as I stand there in fear.

I push my arms against his chest and push back. It's no longer Luke standing in front of me. I look into Tom's dark eyes. He's not wearing his cap like usual. His dark hair is greased back, making him look even more evil than before. A deep smile forms on his face making his leaf-shaped freckles scrunch together.

I try to push him away but his strong grip overpowers me. He grabs me and drags me towards the water. I fall forward into the water and he grabs my head and shoves me under. I panic franticly as I try to lift back up. I shove my hands in the sand and try to push, but his force is too strong. He grabs me by my hair and brings me back up. "If I can get you into another coma, you'll be stuck with me for good."

He shoves me back into the water. I'm suffocating and my lungs feel heavier by the second. My mind begins to fade. I'm going to die. This is my time. My heart starts to slow down and my body becomes numb. I'm fading.

Chapter 14

I wake up to a slap in the face. I take a loud breath as if I'm still drowning. I continuously cough as Luke pats my back. I look up and realize I'm on the floor in Michael's room. I panic and sit up with force. "Michael, where's Michael? Is he ok?"

"Shh, he's ok. He's in his crib." I begin to bawl and fall into Luke's arms.

"I fell asleep with him in my arms. I can't believe I did that. I put him in harm's way again."

He wipes my tears and rubs my head. "I woke up and you weren't next to me and I panicked. I came in here and saw you two sleeping, but your body was shaking. I quickly grabbed Michael and then I saw you stop moving and you'd stopped breathing. I didn't know what to do. I kept shaking and shaking you but you weren't waking up. I'm so sorry I hit you, but I had to wake you up. I almost lost you."

He tightens his arms around me. "Oh my God. I could have hurt my baby."

"You couldn't help it, plus I was here to take care of it. I'm more concerned with the fact that you almost died in my arms. What the hell happened?"

I shake my head and begin to cry again. "The guard didn't kill Tom. He's still alive."

"How are you sure?"

"He showed up in my dream posed as you. He made me think it was you. He told me no one can stop him. He tried to drown me to the point of a coma, not death. Because in a coma is when I'm vulnerable and he can take over. If I die, he'll never have me."

"This can't be," Luke says with despair.

He holds me close as my tears dry. There's nothing left, nothing else I can do. I hear my phone ringing from the bedroom. If someone is calling in the middle of the night, it has to be important. I jump up and rush to the phone.

"Hello?"

"Oh, thank God you're alright," Fredrick says with panic.

"Huh?"

"The plan didn't work. Tom snapped the neck of the guard. I don't know how in the world he's capable of doing something like that, but he's much stronger than I thought."

I stare blankly at the wall as he speaks. Fear, hurt, pain, and worry take over my body and mind. "He's never going to stop."

"I'm so sorry. I'll find another way, even if it means me going in there and shooting him. Because he killed the guard he's now in solitary confinement."

"You're not going to murder anyone. I'm not letting you do that."

"I can go in there wanting to ask questions. I'll be able to be with him alone. There has to be a way around this, and I'm going to do some research."

There's no point in arguing right now. "Alright, just be careful please."

"You do the same. I'd tell you not to go to sleep, but that's impossible. Just stay strong."

"I had a very close call; he almost got me for good. He's getting closer and I don't know how much longer I have or how much more I can take. Luke woke me up as he saw me struggling."

"Let me talk to Luke." I hand Luke the phone. I wish I can hear their conversation.

"I think that's a great idea. Let's start now. Can you send him over?" Oh, no what idea are they coming up with now?

Luke hangs up the phone and sits next to me on the bed. "It's not safe for you to go to bed without someone watching over you to wake you up if you struggle, so Arnold and I are going to take turns watching you while the other sleeps."

"Seriously? I don't need a watch crew. I can take care of myself."

"Dammit Linda, stop being so stubborn! He almost had you, and I almost lost you. We're doing this whether you like it or not."

"I can't stand that I can't control this. I feel so fucking weak and I hate it."

"Stop it," he says grabbing my face and looking into my eyes. "You're not weak. He's a very strong man with strong powers. I'm not taking another risk. You mean everything to me and if something were to happen to you, I'd never forgive myself."

I look away from his eyes in shame. He pulls my head back up. "We're taking these precautions until Fredrick can figure out a way to take care of Tom. I don't care what you think or how you feel about it. I'm keeping you safe."

I nod as tears fall again. He holds me in his arms and doesn't let go. We hear a knock on the door. "Stay here, it's Arnold."

They talk for a few minutes outside in the hallway. "Ok Arnold is going to sleep for two hours while I stay awake and then we're going to switch, since there are only a few hours left until morning."

I look at Arnold who has a smile on his face like usual. "Thank you for agreeing to this, Arnold."

"Don't mention it, Linda, anything to help you all out." Luke shows him to the spare bedroom.

And then Luke comes and tucks me in. "Get some rest. I'll be right here."

My eyes are swollen from crying and they become heavy quickly.

I wake up to the sound of my alarm. Four hours of sleep with no dreams feels pretty good. Luke drops me at work and the line is down the street again. I wonder how long this will go on for. Oh well, it keeps me busy and my mind off of things.

As the day continues, the customers keep on coming, asking questions such as, "What do the dreams feel like? Have you had any recently?" It's starting to get old now.

"Go in the break-room and rest for a while, Linda," Bobby says as he walks out the back room with the lunch tray.

"Thank you, Bobby. I need to feed Michael anyway." The rest of the day goes pretty smoothly. Before I know it Luke walks through the door.

I walk up and give him a kiss. "How was your day?" "Back to back surgeries today. I'm exhausted."

"I bet you are. How about we pick up some food for tonight? I know neither of us feels like cooking."

"Sounds good." I pick up Michael from the crib and place him in my carrier.

"Sarah and Bobby, are you two ok to close up?"

"Absolutely. Go home and get some rest," Sarah says with a comforting smile.

Luke and I head to Ted's Butcherblock for some freshly made sandwiches.

***

The next few days go by quickly. I haven't had any dreams and Tom hasn't shown his face. Maybe the murder attempt scared him off? Wishful thinking, I know. I'm waiting for a call from Sargent Collins today, hoping to hear good news about the kidnappings. I hope they catch the man.

Luke and I are enjoying our steaks for dinner when my phone rings. It's Sargent Collins. "Hello, I've been waiting all day for your call. I hope you have good things to tell me."

"Good evening, Mrs. Jackson. I have great news. Because of your help we were able to catch the man. He ended up grabbing the girl and tried to get away, but my men caught him and no harm was done to the little girl. You were right about everything; what the little girl was wearing, where they were standing when it happened, the exact time, and the description of the mother. I'm a true believer in your gift now and I'm astonished. I'd love to work with you more."

"Thank you for your kind words. I'll be happy to help you on cases where you get stuck and need answers. I'm busy enough here in Charleston as it is. But for cases like this one, where we can talk details over skype or the phone, I'd gladly help."

"That's great news, thank you so much. I'll be in touch. Again, thanks for your help."

"You're welcome." I hang up the phone with a gratifying smile on my face.

"I'm assuming it's good news?"

"Yes. I'm going to keep helping them as well."

"Babe, don't you think that's a little too much?"

"No, because they're only asking for help on cases they have trouble with."

"Alright, whatever you say, but you know you can say no at any time."

"I know."

As we put the dishes in the dishwasher my phone rings again.

It's a number I don't recognize. I decide not to answer it. It goes straight to voicemail. Luke looks over at me as I listen to the voicemail.

His eyebrow rises. "Who was it?"

"A Sargent Bedford form Atlanta PD wanting help on a case." My phone rings again and I stare at it in my hand. Another number I don't recognize.

Luke shakes his head. "Don't answer it. It is getting late." Again I let it go to voicemail and this time it's Chicago PD wanting help. Luke sighs as he walks towards me and grabs my phone. "I'm turning it off for the night. We can use my phone for an alarm. You don't need all this."

How am I going to be able to help everyone? I can't let these cases go. My mind races at a thousand miles. I need to take it one case at a time. I slowly drift into sleep.

I'm walking through a huge crowded mall. I hear many footsteps, chatter, and laughter. I walk around and take a closer look. I'm in the Mall of America. Oh God no, please don't let something big happen here. It's the largest and most well-known mall, and a big tourist attraction. I see something very peculiar; men and women wearing top hats and tons of them. What the fuck is going on?

Then I stop dead in my tracks when I hear scream after scream. I look around and see the people in top hats pull out an AR gun. Each one has the same gun. People are rushing around and panicking. "Attention!" I hear over a microphone and instantaneously every top hat person fires their guns in the air. Glass shatters and people fall over screaming and covering their heads.

I look in the middle of the mall and see the ringleader of the group. He has a gold top hat and a large microphone.

"Everyone ready?" he asks. My heart begins to race. Fuck, ready for what? I look around and see the top hat people move their guns, pointing them at all the innocent people.

No, no please no; so many innocent people, men, women, and children. "Let's have some fun!" says the leader. "FIRREEEEE" he screams into the microphone. I crawl behind a wall. Thousands of shots and splashes of blood come from everywhere. I cover my ears as I hear glass breaking, shots firing, and screams fading. I look down at my phone, it's Saturday at noon. They have no mercy. The top hat people are everywhere, killing everyone in sight. I hear the cop sirens in the distance.

"Time to flee the area!" the leader says. They start to run all together in the same direction throwing their hats to the ground. As I peek around the corner I feel a small knock to the back of my head.

"You don't think you're going to escape now do you?" a soft voice says. I realize they're pointing a gun right at my head. I freeze in fear. I hear them pulling the trigger slowly. I close my eyes, take a deep breath, and prepare for what's coming next.

I twitch and fall to the floor as I hear the gun shot. I sit up on the floor and feel the back of my head. I'm sweating profusely and shaking. My heart won't stop pounding and my breathing is shorter and quicker. Fuck, a panic attack. I can't calm down. Arnold rushes over because Luke is surprisingly still sleeping.

"Linda, Linda what's wrong?" he says as he kneels beside me with his hand on my back. My hand is on my heart, and I can't spit out any words because my breathing is too heavy.

"Luke, get up!" Arnold screams.

Luke rushes over and takes me in his arms. "Shh, relax Linda. Control the attack. Slow your breathing down." He gently rubs my back as I try to calm down. My heart begins slowing its pace but I see black spots forming. They're getting closer and closer together. My head is feeling heavy. Complete darkness.

A cold damp wash cloth pats my face as I slowly come back and open my eyes. I look into Luke's crystal blue eyes. "Did I pass out again?"

He nods. "Yes, you did. You had a pretty intense panic attack."

"Fuck," I say touching my head. I start to get up. "I need to call Fredrick now."

Luke gently pushes me back down. "He can wait. Was it Tom"?

"No, Tom hasn't shown up recently. But hundreds of people are going to die if I don't call Fredrick. I want to call him now," I say with a stern tone.

"No need to call him when I'm right here," Arnold says with a soft tone. "I'll write everything down in my notebook," he says pulling it out of his backpack. "I'll head to the station as soon as you tell me about the dream."

"Oh thank you." I give him all the details.

"Wow, another big case. You keep dreaming these big crimes and every police department in the US is going to want to work with you."

"Trust me, that's what I'm afraid of, but I have to do it."

"I understand. I'll head to the station now and give these details to Fredrick."

***

Saturday comes around and the top hat murders are taken care of before any of the shooting occurs. Tons of cops stroll in and take away the people involved before they can even reach for their guns. Of course, my name is brought up. And once again I appear on the news for helping to save many lives. They show footage of the cops taking away the top hat people in handcuffs. They show my picture on the screen and explain how I saw this happen in my dreams. They call me a hero once again.

"I don't know if I can keep taking this publicity," I say to Luke as I turn off the TV.

"There's not much you can do about it. Eventually it'll die down."

"Yeah, eventually, but who knows how long that will be?" My phone begins to ring. The ringing doesn't seem to stop and voicemail after voicemail is left.

Luke puts his hand out, and I give the phone to him. He turns it off and places it on the kitchen counter. He walks back in, picks me up off the couch, and carries me to the bedroom. He rests me on the bed and climbs on top, looking me deeply in the eyes before kissing me hard and slow. "Let me help you relax and see if I can take some of that stress away."

Chapter 15

A few months have passed and Thanksgiving is about a week away. Michael is finally using a bottle and sleeping through the nights now. I haven't had any dreams about Tom and I'm praying that he has given up. I've been working with different police departments as I receive phone calls. I don't answer all of them or return all of their calls but I try to help as many as I can. My shop is still busy with lines of customers stretching down the street every morning. The press has given me and the shop a rest, which is nice. I'm starting to become comfortable with who I am and what I can do. I enjoy helping and saving people.

As I'm ringing up Jen, one of my regular customers May rushes in with a bubbly smile on her face. She runs up behind the counter and gives me a hug. "Well hey sis, what's going on?"

She pushes out from my hug and giggles as she shows me her hand. I scream out loud and we both jump around in circles like little kids. "My baby sister is getting married everyone!" I yell out for the whole shop to hear. Everyone claps in sync.

"Come here and tell me everything," I say as I pull her into the break room.

"Ok, ok so it happened last night!" she says with pure excitement. I have to calm her down so I can understand what the hell she's saying.

"He took me to a beautiful dinner at High Cotton."

"Wow, fancy dinner. I like where this is going already," I say with a smile.

"Charlie then ordered a fancy bottle of wine and let me order whatever I wanted. We finished off sharing a delicious slice of their oatmeal cream pie. After, he took me to Seabrook Island and we walked hand in hand in the sand as the sun set. He stopped me as we walked and told me how much he loves me, got down

118

on one knee, and asked me to marry him! It was beautiful and I bawled. I didn't see it coming at all."

I tear up a little. "How sweet; I can't believe my baby sister is getting married. I'm so excited for you."

"Will you be my maid of honor?"

"Uh yeah, of course I will! When's the big day?"

"April 24th of this year!"

"Wow, that's so soon!"

"I know but we didn't want to wait and it's going to be very small; just our immediate families. His brother is going to be his best man and neither of us is inviting anyone else, so it'll be just you and him up there with us."

"Sounds like it'll be wonderful. Do you know where you want to have it yet?"

"Yeah, we talked about it last night. We want to have it on the beach. We're going to talk to Seabrook Island Club about having the wedding on the beach and then the reception inside the club."

"That'll be beautiful."

"I want you and Mom to come dress shopping with me this weekend!"

"I can't wait!"

I begin the closing down process with Sarah and Bobby. As we finish up someone knocks on the door. I see Fredrick's tall body standing in front of the door. "Hey, what's going on? You usually call if something is up. Is everything ok?"

"Yeah, can we have a seat real quick?" I feel nervous as we head to the table. He usually calls if he needs help with a case, but this time something is different. He doesn't seem as sure and confident as usual.

"Ok, you're freaking me out. What is it?"

"Tyler is dead. His body was found by Waterfront Park Fountain this morning."

My heart is pounding but I'm not sure if it's a rush of excitement, panic, or relief. "Oh my God. Do you know who did it?"

"There was a note left on his body." He slowly pulls out a piece of paper from his pocket.

I take the note and it reads. "This is a gift to Linda, one less person to harm you, one step closer to getting what's mine."

"Who the fuck would do this?" I cry out as tears fall.

"I think that whoever is working for Tom in our precinct did this as a message from Tom to you."

"But Tom hasn't shown up in any of my dreams. I've been doing so well for these past few months."

"Honestly Linda, I think he's playing one big game. He wants your guard to be down so the next time he attacks, it'll be for good."

"Fredrick, what should I do? I'm so scared."

"Call Luke and have him meet us down here. He needs to know what's going on. You didn't happen to dream about the death of Tyler did you?"

"No, I didn't."

"There's Tom's influence. I believe this is his way of telling us that he's in total control."

"Fuck," I say as I call Luke. "He's on his way. What are we going to do about this?"

"I'm going in there today to see Tom, check out the security system, and see if there's a way I can get in and finish him for good. I'm going to threaten Tom to leave you alone and if he doesn't then he'll die."

"I don't think threatening him will do any good."

"I don't think so either, but it gives me a chance to scope out the place and create a plan."

Luke storms through the door. "What's going on?"

"Tyler is dead," Fredrick says flat out.

"Really? Well that's one out of the way," Luke responds with no sympathy.

I hand Luke the note. "This was found on the body."

Luke crumples the note in his hand and slams it on the table. "This is Tom's doing, isn't it?"

Fredrick responds quickly, "Yes, I believe so."

"Months have passed with no sign or word from Tom. Why all of a sudden?"

"To throw me off track and make it easier for him to get to me. At least that's what Fredrick and I think."

"What are you going to do about it?" Luke asks Fredrick as he sits across from us. Fredrick begins explaining what we already discussed.

"Alright, the sooner it's done the better. I don't want it to be too late. We should start watching Linda again at night and make sure she wakes up if needed."

I roll my eyes as Fredrick agrees with Luke. "It's for your own protection," Fredrick exclaims.

"I know, I know."

"Alright, well you two get home safely and I'm going to pay Tom a little visit now. I'll call you soon."

"Great thanks," I say as I push in my chair. I look down at my watch. "We need to get home. Mom is watching Michael and I'm sure she's tired."

"See you all tomorrow," I yell to Sarah and Bobby.

"See ya girl. If you need anything let us know," replies Sarah.

Luke grabs my hand as we walk out the door. "So babe, what do you want for dinner tonight?"

"I'm craving some good ole fettuccini alfredo."

"Mmm, sounds great to me."

We walk inside the house and Mom is holding Michael tight in her arms as they watch TV. She's feeding him a bottle. "Well hello you two," she says with her bright smile.

"Sorry we're late. We had some business to take care of."

She shakes her head and smiles, her dangling butterfly earrings swinging from side to side. "You know, it's not a problem. It's just more time with my lovely grandson. Is everything ok?"

"Yeah, nothing to worry about, Mom. It's time to take care of Tom for good this time."

"It better be. We're all ready for him to be taken care of. You'll still be able to make it to Thanksgiving dinner this Saturday, right? I know the entire family would love to meet the new baby!"

"Of course we'll be there."

"Great, I'll be back over tomorrow morning to watch Michael before you go to work."

"Thank you so much for doing this, Mom. You're saving us a ton of money by watching him every day."

She kisses me on the forehead. "You already know what I'm going to say, honey."

"Now let me see my baby boy," I say as I grab him and kiss him.

After our wonderful dinner that Luke whipped up we decide to watch some TV. My cell phone rings and its Fredrick. I wasn't expecting his call until later.

"Hey, how did it go?"

"Well you were right about threatening him not fazing him whatsoever. He's ruthless and strong. Good thing is, once you get in to his cell, security is nothing. They don't seem to care as much about the criminals in solitary confinement. If I can catch him off guard while he's sleeping, and keep it quiet with a cut to the throat, it shouldn't be a problem."

"Are you sure about this? You're taking a big risk."

"This man doesn't deserve to breathe. I'm positive. I'm going to wait until after the holiday, early next week. I want to think up a good plan to get away with this smoothly. I do know another guard who's going to help me out. He's going to make sure no one goes into that area until after I leave."

"Alright, I hope that won't be too late."

He sighs into the phone. "If you have another dream about him before my plan then I'll do it earlier."

"Ok, that sounds good. Thank you for taking care of this."

"You can thank me when it's done. Have a good night. Arnold is on his way over now."

"Thank you." I tell Luke everything he says. He puts Michael down for bed and moments later Arnold is at the door. Luke decides to take first watch and let Arnold sleep.

I lie in bed hoping and praying that Tom doesn't make his way into my dreams tonight. I close my eyes as they become heavy.

I'm in a dark, cold cement room. I can't see anything, but I hear drops of water in the distance. It's warm and musty in here and smells like dirty clothes. Where am I? I move around to see if I can find my phone and get some light. As I grab my phone from my pocket I hear a soft whisper.

"Is somebody there? Please help me." The whisper is soft and shaky. This woman is scared.

"Yes, my name is Linda. I can help you."

"Oh, thank God. I'm in so much pain and I'm so scared that he's going to come back."

"Who is he?" I turn on the flashlight on my phone.

"He's a bad man," she whispers back. I look around the room and become sick at what I see through the dim light. Five women handcuffed to the cement wall. Their clothes are completely ripped. Their hair is damp and greasy from sweat and dirt. They're pale and malnourished. I can't tell if they're alive or not. Their heads are hanging down and there's no movement. I glance over as I see one

woman lift her head.

"Over here," she tries to speak up. "We need help. I feel like I'm going to die."

I walk slowly over to her. "Who's the man?"

"He calls himself The Warrior. He beats us and uses us for his pleasure. He doesn't feed us or give us anything to drink. I haven't heard those first two women speak in a day. We're all going to die in here."

"Ok, I'm going to help you. Do you have any idea where we are?"

"I was drugged when he kidnapped me. I was loopy but I remember glancing out of the car window as we were pulling in. My vision was blurry but I remember seeing a stop sign and a one way sign. Then I got a glance at the street name, Atlantic Street, and then the car stopped. When he opened up the door and saw that my eyes were open, I remember feeling a sharp pain, and I woke up in here."

"That's great. What did the man look like?"

"He was wearing a white surgical mask and scrubs. He's a tall black man and is extremely muscular."

She becomes quiet as we hear footsteps from above. "Fuck, he's coming back. I don't know how much longer I can make it."

I whisper back as the footsteps start coming closer. "Try to fight it. I'll get help right away. Stay strong."

I hear the door begin to creak open and shut my eyes tightly. "Wake up Linda, wake up." The light from the door floods in. I can't seem to wake up. I open my eyes and see the tall man standing in the light. I drop my mouth when I see who is standing in front of me.

I gasp. "Jeff."

***

I wake up taking in a big breath. Luke perks up immediately and so does Arnold. I'm breathing heavily and my hand is on my heart. I can feel it pounding in my chest. *I can't believe that was Jeff. Luke's best friend, his brother, this can't be. How am I going to tell Luke?* My eyes are wide open in shock. I look over at Luke, into his blue eyes, about to break his heart.

"Baby, what's wrong? You're scaring me."

"It can't be," I say shaking my head. "This must be a mistake."

"What, what is it?"

I explain the dream, where the women are, and what's being done to them. "We need to get Fredrick and leave right away,"

123

says Arnold.

"There's more to the story or else you wouldn't be freaking out as much as you are," Luke says with caution.

"It's the man who's doing this. I saw him right before I woke up."

"Who is it?"

I swallow before I can get the name out. "I-it was Jeff," I say in slow motion.

"Jeff? As in my best friend, Jeff? As in the one whom I work with every day? You must have made a mistake."

"Trust me, Luke. I'm hoping it's a mistake, but I know I saw him." He stares into space, wide eyed, with no expression.

"I'm sorry guys, but I'm calling Fredrick now." I rub Luke on the back as he sits in silence, shock, and fear.

"I trusted him like family and I let him near you. What if he'd hurt you? I'd have never forgiven myself."

"Shh Luke, he didn't hurt me. I'm fine."

"That lying, betraying, fucking bastard. Wait until I get my hands on him."

"Luke, don't be stupid." He gets up fast and puts on a shirt. "I'm going to confront him."

"Oh no you're not," Arnold says as he walks into the room. "I just got off the phone with Fredrick. He's gathering a crew and heading over there. There are a ton of houses on Atlantic Street. They're going to search every house until they find that basement."

"No need to search. Jeff owns a rental property on Atlantic Street. He always told me a family of four was living there. That fucking liar."

"What's the address?"

"I'll show you. I want to see it for myself. I want to see who Jeff really is."

"I'm going with you," I say quickly. "I'll call May and Charlie to come over and watch Michael."

"Ok, we leave in ten minutes. I'll tell Fredrick to come here and we'll all go over together," says Arnold as he dials the number.

It doesn't take long for May and Charlie to come by. "Are you going to be ok?" May asks me with concern.

"I'm fine. I'm more worried about Luke right now."

"Take care of Luke. Michael will be in good hands."

I hug both May and Charlie. "Thank you both."

"Alright, they're here, we need to go," says Arnold. Luke rushes out the door without saying a word. I've never seen Luke like this before. I walk out and see Luke and Fredrick talking. I walk over to hear what's going on.

"I'm going to ride with Fredrick, you stay with Arnold. Don't get out of the car for any reason," Luke says with anger.

I nod in agreement. I'm not sure how to act right now. I'm afraid to see how Luke is going to react when he sees that it's Jeff. It's a silent car ride up to Atlantic Street. I wish I could be in the car with Luke.

We pull up next to the house. It's still somewhat dark out, and the sun is slowly rising. The cops rush out of their cars with guns and quickly surround the house. Luke stands right on the sidewalk leading to the front door, waiting. Two cops break open the front door and more storm in and follow behind. I stay in the car as ordered, but roll the window down to listen.

They call an ambulance, which is ready if necessary. About five minutes later a few cops walk out carrying bodies. The same women I saw with ripped clothes. "We need some help in here," one of the officers yells out. The paramedics rush into the house and bring out the remaining women. The last one they carry out is the same woman I spoke with.

I get out of the car and walk over to them. "Are they alive?"

The paramedic responds in a soft tone. "Barely. Two of them didn't make it, but three did. We're talking them to the hospital now."

I tear up as I walk back towards the car. I turn around and see Fredrick leading the man responsible for all of this in handcuffs. The man lifts his head and looks at Luke standing in front of them.

Luke stares at the man who he thought was his brother, who supported him, and trusted him. He stares coldly into Jeff's eyes. I stand there in shock as I see tears fall from Jeff's face. Luke shakes his head and punches Jeff hard in the face knocking him to his knees. He's about to hit him again when Fredrick yells out for him to stop.

"How could you? Who the fuck are you?"

"I'm sorry, Luke. I can't help myself. I'm sick. I hate that it took everything in my power not to hurt Linda. But I couldn't do that to you, man."

I raise my eyebrows in surprise at what he had said. Luke punches him hard again. "I hope you rot in prison, you sick bastard." Jeff's head hangs as Fredrick gets him back off his feet and walks him to the back of a police car.

Luke doesn't move from where he stands. I slowly walk up to him. "Baby, I'm so sorry." He takes me in his arms and begins to cry.

Chapter 16

The next few days seem to go by in slow motion. Luke hasn't been the same since the incident with Jeff, which I understand. I know what it feels like to get hurt by someone you thought was close to you. We have to pull ourselves together before we arrive at my parent's house for Thanksgiving. Everyone will be excited to see the new baby; we have to act like we're happy.

As I drive, Luke remains quiet. "Are you sure you're up to this, babe? I can take you home and just go with Michael. I can tell everyone that you're not feeling good."

He shakes his head. "No, I'll be fine. I think being with the family will be a good thing for me. If I'm alone that'll only make me think harder."

"Ok, baby," I say, rubbing his leg. I glance over at him. "I love you."

"I love you too," he says with a small smile. That's the first time I've seen him smile in days.

When we walk in we're bombarded with compliments towards Michael. Everyone wants to hold him. My Aunt takes Michael and I head over to greet May and Charlie. "How's Luke doing?" May whispers to me as we part our hugs.

"He's alright, still pretty upset."

"We've all been there," May replies. Isn't that the truth? It's sad that so many terrible things have happened to this family in only a matter of two years.

The night turns into laughter and family games, not to mention the alcohol and amazing food. Luke is laughing and having a good time. May announces her engagement and they all go crazy!

By the time we get home, we're all exhausted and head straight to bed.

Monday morning comes around quickly. I head to the station

to speak with Fredrick before going into work. I want to make sure that today is the day he puts a knife to Tom's throat.

As I get ready to turn the corner to walk into Fredrick's office I stop when I hear him speaking with someone. I stand quietly to listen. "We really need her help. We've heard miracle stories about her. Is it true?" The voice of the man is someone's I don't recognize.

"Why should I tell you anything? She has been through a lot and doesn't need the added stress." That's definitely Fredrick's voice.

"I understand that, but this case has been open for three months and we still can't find the killer. She's our last resort to catch this guy."

"I'll contact her today and will try, but I can't promise anything." I decide to step in and interrupt.

"What do you need my help with?" I say as I enter the office. Fredrick looks surprised as I walk in. I hold out my hand to shake hands with a short bulky man. "I'm Linda Jackson, the one you're requesting to help you out."

"It's an honor to meet you," he says as he shakes my hand. "My name is Sargent Blooms and I'm with the Miami Police Department."

I raise an eyebrow. "As in Miami, Florida?"

"Yes ma'am."

"Wow, word travels fast," I say with surprise.

"I've been paying attention to the news. You're the new big thing in the FBI department. Everyone wants a chance to work with you."

"Thank you. So what do you need help with?" Fredrick looks over at me and shakes his head from side to side, but so slowly that it's almost unnoticeable. I nod to let him know it's ok.

"Really? You'll help us?"

"Depending on the case, how much you already know, and what information you need."

He motions for me to have a seat. "This killer has been at it for three months now and each week there's a new murder. He has a pattern but it's a tough one. His victims are all involved with different insurance companies around Miami. There's no specific gender or age that he prefers. The only thing connecting the twelve victims so far are that they work at different insurance companies."

"Ok, so this guy obviously has had issues with insurance in the past. Something must have really ticked him off. How does he murder them and what time of day usually?" Fredrick listens and takes notes as we speak to one another.

"So far we've found the bodies in dumpsters near the insurance companies they work for. The time of murder varies and we don't know where he's committing the murders. He kills them with a single gunshot to the head."

"So why don't you gather up people to watch the insurance company buildings?"

"Do you know how many different insurance companies, let alone people, that work for those companies in Miami? There are tons and this man has no pattern. He's all over the place."

"Ok, wow and there are no leads or suspects at all?"

"Nope. We're not even sure if it's a man. We just assume it is."

"Which insurance company was attacked last? I might be able to go back in time and watch it happen."

"You can do that?"

"It's only happened a few times, but if I really concentrate, I might able to do it."

"Wow, that's great. It was Neighbors Insurance Company; one of their local insurance companies. This killer hits big companies and smaller companies. It was a female agent by the name of Lucy Gilmore. She was 35, Caucasian, and married with two kids. She was murdered three days ago. So we have about a week until his next victim to try and solve this case."

"Ok, I'll see what I can do."

"There's a catch."

I raise an eyebrow in suspicion. "What is it?"

"We may need to you to come to Miami. We can fly you out and back for free and put you up in a nice hotel."

"Oh, no way. I can't do that. I have an almost six month old baby and there's no way that he's up for traveling. I've helped many other police departments in different states from here. I don't have to be near the places where the murders occur. My dreams are strong and well controlled."

"Ok, I can stay one more day and night here. Do you think you can find any information out before then?"

"I can try, but I can't promise anything. Do you have photos of the victims and the insurance companies?"

He pulls twelve files out from his black, leather briefcase. "Yes, I have them all here."

"Great, let me take a look." I put the newest case, Lucy, in the back to review hers last. He's right; they were all shot in the head and a variety of male and female, ages 20-60. I pull out Lucy's file last and take a look; a very pretty girl with long, brown, straight hair. I concentrate on the images of her and the insurance company, paying special attention to the details around the building.

After a few minutes of review I give him back the files. "Thank you. I think that's all I need. I'll do some research on google maps tonight. I can get a good sense of the location and what it looks like from there. I'll try and put myself at the insurance company three days ago to see if I can pinpoint where the murder happens and get a look at the murderer."

"Great, thank you Linda. I appreciate your time and help. Here's my card. Give me a call when you have something. I'll be staying at the King Charles Inn until Wednesday morning. Fredrick sees him out of the door and then shuts it.

"Doing alright?"

"Yes, I'm fine. I enjoy helping with cases as long as I can help from home."

"Agreed. I don't think making a trip to Miami is the best thing for you right now, especially with the whole Tom thing going on. It's safe for you here with Luke, myself, and this department."

"So tonight is the night, right?"

"Yeah, I already have things set and ready for action. The guard is going to call me once Tom is asleep and then I'll go in with my silencer and put a bullet through his head."

I get chills through my body thinking of Tom dead and how much of a stress free life I'll have.

"Great. Will you let me know in the morning?"

"Of course," he says as we walk out the door. I begin to walk away when he calls over, "It'll all be over tonight." I smile in return to his smile. When I turn around from his glare I see one of the police officers looking at Fredrick with wide eyes. Something Fredrick said got under his skin.

Someone on the outside giving me information. I hear Tom's voice in my mind. I wonder if the cop has anything to do with that? The look on his face reveals suspicion. I glance at the cop's name badge. Bridges is his last name.

As soon as I walk out of the building I call Fredrick and give him the name of the cop and explain how he perked up when he heard him say it will all be over tonight. Fredrick is going to keep a close eye on him. I think we just caught the guy who's feeding Tom information!

As I pull into my parking spot at work I see the line outside the door. I can't believe that after all these months we're still just as busy. Of course it doesn't help that when murder cases are solved they mention Linda Jackson and the Charleston Police Department. It seems that the day after cases are solved the line always gets bigger. But today there are only about ten people standing in line outside.

I call Luke's cell phone at midday to check on him. It rings a few times then goes straight to voicemail. I try to call again and this time it goes straight to voicemail. I stare at the phone with confusion. I know he's upset still, but I didn't think he'd ignore my calls. I call over to Sarah as she's making coffee. "Hey, do you mind if you and Bobby take over for the rest of the day. I'm going to the hospital to check on Luke. I have a weird feeling."

"Absolutely hun, we've got it taken care of."

"Great, thanks so much," I say as I kiss her on the cheek and head out the door.

I pull into the visitor's parking lot of the Orthopedic Building at MUSC. I've only been here a few times and still struggle to find my way around. To be honest, I hate hospitals, as they make me nervous.

I walk up to the receptionist and she smiles as she sees me. "Linda, what a nice surprise! It's good to see you again. How are things?" For some reason her curly blonde hair, blue eyes, and big boobs annoy the hell out of me.

"Uh hi, doing well. I'm here to check on Luke. Is he in a case?" I say with a short tone.

Her smile fades. "He already left. He finished his last case and decided to go home."

"This early?" I glance at the clock behind her head. "Did he say where he was going?"

"Just said he was heading home for the day. Is there a problem?"

"No, thank you." I walk quickly out of the door. I try to call

Luke again, and again it goes straight to voicemail. *Where is he? What's going on?*

I drive home in a panic hoping he's there. I pull into the driveway and his car isn't there. I sit there holding the wheel as tears start to form. *Think, where would Luke go to clear his head?* "The pier!" I say out loud. "I bet he's at the pier at Waterfront Park."

When I arrive I see a man sitting at the end, dangling his feet. I walk closer and see that it is indeed Luke. I slowly walk up to him and touch his shoulder. He doesn't flinch. I sit next to him and gently caress his thigh, looking into his tearful eyes. He doesn't look back into mine. I move his chin to face me. "Baby, are you alright? I'm worried about you."

He looks me in the eyes as tears slowly fall down his cheeks. He then hugs me tight with his face buried into my upper chest. I rub his head and hold him. "It's ok baby, I'm here." A few minutes later he raises his head to meet my eyes.

"He was my brother, the only man I ever trusted, more so than my own father."

"I know baby and I'm so sorry. I wish I knew what to say to help."

"I already have a hard time trusting people and now this? I don't know if I can trust anyone ever again."

I look him deep in the eyes grabbing his face. "Baby, you can trust me. I'd never do anything to hurt you."

"I know you wouldn't. Linda, you're the only one I can say I truly trust and the only one I'll continue to trust. I don't know what I'd do without you and I never want to find out."

"Don't worry, baby. You won't have to."

"I promise to protect you until the day I die."

I smile at his comment and he kisses me softly on the lips. "I love you more than life itself, Luke."

"There are no words to describe how much I love you, Linda. How did you know I was here?"

"Well, I was freaking out because your phone was going straight to voicemail and you never turn off your phone. So I left work and went to the hospital and the receptionist told me you'd left already. I was surprised because you usually text me if you leave early. I came home and your car wasn't there so I thought of where you'd to clear your head, and here you are!"

"You know me so well. I'm sorry about not answering your phone calls. My phone battery died. I figured if I came here I'd get home in time to meet you. I'm sorry that I scared you. Thank you for coming here. Just seeing your smile helps me."

"Of course, Luke. I'll always be here for you." He brings me into his arms and I rest my head on his shoulder. We look into the beautiful ocean and cherish this moment. On the way home I update him on the meeting with Sargent Blooms. Luke is becoming increasingly supportive, helping on the different cases and working with different police departments.

"You know, I've been thinking; I may hand my shop over to Sarah and Bobby and work full time with the FBI."

Luke shoots a quick look at me. "What? But you love your coffee shop. It's your life."

"I know, I do love it, but look how much money I'm bringing in for working with the FBI. Just think if I did this full time?"

"True, but what if working on too many different cases at once causes your health issues to return or worsen, then what will you do?"

"I guess I never thought about that. But I haven't had too many outbreaks in a while. I can now stop the flashes and attacks when I feel them coming on."

"But look what happens to you when you can't control them in time. It can be life threatening."

"I guess you're right. But the more practice I have with the dreams and working these cases, the better I'll be at controlling those outbreaks. It's something I'm going to deal with whether I work full time or help out with cases here and there. It's just a matter of me controlling the flashes to the point to where they don't bother me."

"And you think working more cases and getting more practice will help with that?"

"Yes, look how far I've come already."

He nods his head. "I see your point. I just think it's too early to give up your shop and work full time on cases, at least until the Tom situation is taken care of for good."

"Ok, I can do that."

After putting Michael down for bed, we both decide to shower. There's no better picture than Luke standing naked with water dripping down his muscular body. After the shower we lie in bed and talk to each other. We talk about memories from our wedding and honeymoon, and how we need to take a big family vacation this summer with my parents, May and Charlie, and the three of us. "That would be so much fun. May will be a newlywed by then. We'll make sure to play around their honeymoon."

"I'm so glad May found someone as good as Charlie. After everything she went through, I'm glad she can finally settle down," Luke says.

"Me too, I've never seen her that happy." We talk a little more until our eyes become heavy.

Neighbors Insurance is the building I'm standing right in front of. I look at my phone to see the date. It's Friday, so basically three days ago. Perfect, now I have to go in and find Lucy and keep a watch out. I see a woman that looks like the one from the picture. Her long brown straight hair falls neatly over her shoulders. She has a bright, wide smile, and beautiful green eyes. I can't help but feel pain for her.

"Hello, Miss, may I help you with something?" she calls over to me.

"Um," shit I didn't think of what I was going to say. "Yes, a friend of mine recommended this company along with a Lucy Gilmore?"

She walks out front behind the counter. She's taller than what I expected, so she must have played volleyball. "Why that's me. What can I help you with today?"

"I'm shopping for car insurance. I was wondering if you could give me some information about what you have to offer here."

"I'd be delighted to." She motions over to me to take a seat in her office. We discuss plans and I take her card. She's definitely passionate about her job.

"Great, thank you Lucy. I'll be in touch." If only she knew what was coming. I stake outside the building for the day. I see men and women coming in and out; too many people to remember let alone find anyone suspicious. My vision fixes on a woman in a long sleeve black shirt and a toboggan. It might be the end of November but in Miami the weather is still warm. Something seems off about her. She has long red hair flowing from her toboggan, but it seems dyed. When she walks into the store I pay close attention.

I wake up quickly when my phone goes off. "Fuck!" I yell out. Luke wakes up instantly, too. I answer the phone with anger.

"Hello?"

"Linda, it didn't happen." Fredrick sounds upset.

"What do you mean it didn't happen? You had it all set up."

"Yeah and when I walked in there to shoot him, he was gone. Someone had fucking moved him. Someone knew I was coming."

"You have got to be kidding me!"

"I bet it was Bridges. After you called me I kept an eye on him and for the rest of the day he kept glancing over at me. He must have known we were coming."

"What are you going to do about this now?"

"I'm going to talk to Bridges first thing in the morning. Then talk to the guard and find out where the hell he is."

"You don't think he's out of the prison do you?"

"No way could anyone let him loose, no matter how powerful they are. I'll take care of this. I know I sound like a broken record, but I made a promise and I intend to keep it."

"Ok, keep me posted," I say with a sigh. I'm not that scared anymore, I'm just pissed. How can Tom be so powerful and keep getting away?

Luke looks at me in concern. "Tom is never going to stop," I say.

Chapter 17

"How the fuck does this keep happening? How can he keep getting away with this shit?" Luke says with anger and frustration. "What's Fredrick going to do?"

"He has a lead on someone at the station who's feeding Tom information. He's going to talk to him and the guard at the jail. He's going to try again and keep trying until Tom is dead."

"I hope that's soon."

"You're telling me. I hate falling asleep not knowing what's in store for me through the night. It sucks because I was just finding out information about the case from Miami as soon as he called! I hope I can fall back asleep and end up where I left off. I got a slight glimpse of who might be the killer."

"Well, I'm already up and too pissed off to go back to bed, so I'll let Arnold sleep. I'll keep an eye on you."

"Ok, I love you."

"Love you too and I hope you find something out." I close my eyes and begin to think.

Don't let Tom scare you away from this dream. Stay focused and put yourself right back where you left off, I tell myself to keep on track.

I close my eyes and think of the images from where I was and the woman I saw just before I woke up.

I'm sitting in my car keeping a close eye out for the lady with the red hair. She walks back out from the insurance building and heads towards a car parked on the side of the road. I get a quick look at her face. She has very bushy brown eyebrows and what looks like a big mole right above her lip. She gets into a black Cadillac. I watch from my rearview mirror. She doesn't move an inch. She's waiting for something or someone; Lucy maybe?

Time passes slowly as I watch from behind and to the side to see when Lucy walks out. It's getting dark out. It has to be time for closing. Just then Lucy comes strolling out of the building, walking as if she just kissed the love of her life. She looks so happy, I hate what is about to happen.

Lucy gets into her silver minivan and the black car behind me turns on their engine and lights. Well, I guess she's after Lucy. This woman must be the killer. Lucy pulls her car out and begins to drive. The woman follows her and I follow the woman. How is she going to pull this off?

After a few miles of driving Lucy pulls into a driveway, which I assume is her house. The black car parks on the street, the lights are turned off, and it waits. Lucy gets out of the car and the woman does also. Lucy shuffles her keys to find the house key and the woman quickly gains ground.

The red-haired woman is now standing directly behind Lucy. She must have said something because Lucy turns around slowly. Then BAM, one quick shot to her head and Lucy falls to the ground. The woman looks around to see if there is any movement. She picks up the limp body and carries it to her car. The trunk is open but I can't see what's going on.

I don't see the woman now. Where could she have gone? POW! I hear a loud bang on my driver's side window. She slams the gun into my window and motions for me to roll it down. How the hell did she get here without me seeing? Without hesitation I slam on the gas and watch her fall to the ground from my side mirror. After a while of driving I pull off to the side. I have the ID of the killer, but I have no idea who she's going to attack next.

My head pounds with pain. I hear echoing from behind me as if the voice is coming from my back seat. "Almost there, Linda." The sound of Tom's raspy and eerie voice sends chills down my spine. I can feel my heartbeat in my head as it pounds with pain. I put my hands on my head. "Stop, stop." I shake my head for some relief. "Wake up, Linda, wake up!" I scream out.

I awake with panic as Luke continues to shake me. "I'm alright babe," I say waving my arms and motioning him to stop. About thirty seconds later my alarm goes off. I roll over to turn it off and send a text to Sargent Blooms. "Meet me at my coffee shop, Sweet N' Spice, at 8:00am. I have some information."

"So what happened?" Luke asks. I explain the dream and how Tom appeared right at the end.

"Fredrick needs to do something right now," he says picking up his phone.

"Are you calling him?"

"Yes, to let him know you had a dream. He needs to complete his task by tonight. I'm not risking one more night with your dreams."

"Ok, good idea."

Arnold heads out as soon as we finish breakfast. "I'm taking you and picking you up from work today," Luke says with concern.

Sargent Blooms comes through the door at exactly 8:00am. "Hi, Sargent Blooms, welcome to my coffee shop. Can I get you a coffee before we start?"

"Yes, please. I'll have a large regular coffee, black."

I walk over to where he's sitting and hand him the coffee. He pulls out his notebook and prepares to write down the information. "Ok, tell me what you have."

"Well, it's not a lot, but it's a start."

"Anything will help." I explain about the woman and what she looked like. "I wish I could tell you when she was going to attack next, but she's definitely the killer. She has a very distinct look and shoots these people at their own homes."

"I'm calling it in right now to put out a search for this woman. If we can get a track on her then the problem is solved."

"I'll try to find out more information tonight."

"Sounds good. I'm here until tomorrow morning."

"Great, enjoy your coffee," I say as I head back behind the counter to ring up our line of customers. I glance over at him as he speaks constantly on his phone. I sure hope that was enough information.

As I take a short break and eat a chocolate chip scone I receive a text from Luke. "Hey babe, I'll be running a little late. I'll pick you up as soon as I can. Please don't walk home alone."

***

As I begin the closing down process I receive a phone call from Fredrick. "Hey Linda, I need you to come down to the station."

"Ok, I'll head down now."

"See you soon," he says then hangs up.

"Hey Bobby, would you care to drop me off at the police station real quick?"

"No problem. Let me finish cleaning this tray then we can

head out."

"Thank you!" I send Luke a text to pick me up at the station instead.

I see Fredrick talking with Arnold as I walk into the station. Fredrick waves me to come into his office. Before I enter I see Officer Bridges packing up stuff from his desk into a box.

"Did you fire him?"

"Yup, sure did. I put that disgusting liar through a lie detector test and he failed miserably. He's the one who has been feeding him information." We both shut our mouths when Bridges walks in and sets his badge on his desk.

He glares at me as he walks slowly out of the door, then grins and walks away. My heart begins to race. "Are you sure it's safe for him to be let go?"

"I can't really do much. Our AD is going to try and pin something on him but he probably won't do much time. Do you know how difficult it'll be to play this up in court? Yes we have the lie detector test results but no witnesses. He didn't harm anyone."

"But he fed information to a killer."

"Like I said, our AD will handle it as best as he can. We don't have enough to hold him here yet."

"Ok, is there anything else you need me for?"

"I need your help on a small case. Since I'm going to take care of Tom tonight, I need the extra help."

"Ok, what is it?"

"A mother came in today claiming that her ex-husband, who's a druggy and cooks meth in a house, stole their eight year old daughter. She doesn't know where the house is. I need your help on finding the location."

"Ok, what's the address of the house the mom lives in? If I can dream back to him taking the daughter, then I can follow him to the house they're now at." He gives me the address and shows me a picture of the mom, ex-husband, and the daughter."

"Ok, this shouldn't be too hard. I'll work on it tonight." My phone goes off and I look at it. "Luke is on his way. I'm going to head outside and clear my head until he gets here."

"Ok, want me to come with you?"

"No, I'll be alright."

"Ok, thank you for coming down. We'll be in touch."

I walk outside and stand near the building. I glance into the sky as the sun starts to fall. What a beautiful evening. I hear two men talking around the corner of the building. "It's going to happen tonight." My ears perk up and I walk closer to get a better listen.

"How's it going down?" the other man replies.

"The guard working with Tom is going to give him an IV that will put him in a coma. Once he's in the coma he'll have total control over Linda."

"That's fucking awesome! Tom will finally get what he's been wanting." My knees begin to shake and buckle. *How many people does Tom have on his side? It seems never ending.*

I walk across the street hoping they won't see me, and I wait for Luke impatiently. The cops are starting to head home for the evening and the area quickly empties. I get out my phone and call Fredrick to tell him what I just heard. "Linda, are you ok?"

"Not really, I just overheard-" Then BAM, there's an instant and sharp pain to the back of my head followed by nothing but darkness.

Chapter 18

My head throbs as I slowly move my head and open my eyes. My vision is blurry but I see dim light above me. The sharp pain intensifies when I receive a hard slap to my face. I slowly lift my head when I see a blurry face right in front of me. The face seems familiar but I can't fully identify the man yet.

"Bet you didn't see this one coming, you psychic bitch!" he says with a vengeful voice. I'm finally able to see clearly and I stare at the man in front of me.

"Bridges?" I say softly.

"Why, you do remember me! You're the one who made me lose my job."

"I didn't mean for that to happen."

"Oh, don't patronize me, you bitch. It just so happens that Tom and I have plans for you."

I try to move around when I realize that my hands and legs are tied to bed posts. I pull my arms hard, seeing if I can escape, but there's no use. "Oh trust me, you won't be getting out. I've tied you up nice and tight."

"Why are you doing this? What did I ever do to you?"

"Well, I just did Tom's dirty work for him for no reason. I didn't give two shits about who you were or what so-called talent you have, but after getting fired because of you, I grew more interested."

"So your Tom's lapdog, huh?" Another hard hit to the face. I taste blood in my mouth and spit it out towards Bridges.

"You're trying to act all big and tough now?"

"Someone will find me."

"No one will be able to find you." I glance down in my jeans and realize my cell phone is in my pocket. I hope to God Fredrick can track this phone.

Bridges glances at his watch. "It's almost that time! As soon as I get the text from the guard that he has been put into the coma, it'll be your turn." he says holding a needle in his hand.

Show no fear, Linda. See if you can play games with his head. "Do you really have the balls to put that needle in my arm? You do realize that once Fredrick comes through that door, you'll be locked up for life and you won't have any freedom."

"Don't think you can try and scare me out of doing this, as it won't work." There's something in his voice. Hesitation maybe?

"Let me ask you this...did you realize that my cell phone is sitting in my pocket?" He rolls his eyes upwards as if thinking about what I just said. I smile in response. "Oh, so you didn't? Which means my husband and Fredrick will be able to track where we are."

He laughs. "Oh, whatever! Just stop fucking talking." He puts duct tape over my mouth, slaps me around the face again, and throws my phone on the floor smashing the screen.

Please Luke and Fredrick, help me. Bridges gets a phone call. His head moves up and down as he listens intently. "Alright, it's set in stone. I have the needle ready. I'll call when it's done."

Fuck, when what's done? What's he going to do to me? He walks over to me in what seems like slow motion holding the needle up as if I'm in a horror movie. He's grinning from ear to ear. "Are you ready for everything to end? Are you ready to be Tom's forever?"

Tears fall from my eyes, my heart is pounding fast, and my hands are shaking. He sits down next to me in his rolling chair and rips the tape off of my mouth. "Any last words before I insert this needle and it's all over?"

I glare at him. "Fuck you."

He laughs with an eerie pitch. "Oh, you crack me up. Have fun on the other side." He puts the needle closer to my arm.

"You won't get away with this. Even if this is the end for me, you'll never be free; I just want you to know that."

"Yeah right." The needle is right in front of my vein. "Sleep tight," he says, laughing. I take a deep breath to prepare myself for the end. He's about to insert the needle when the front door to the room opens.

"Thank God!" I yell out with tears. Bridges turns his chair around so quickly he almost falls out of it. Fredrick and Luke are standing in the doorway, both with guns.

"Get the fuck up and put your hands in the air," Fredrick says with anger. Luke rushes over to me.

"Oh baby, I'm so sorry," he says kissing me many times. He unties my arms and legs and pulls me in close to him.

Fredrick throws Bridges up against the wall slamming his face. He wraps his wrists in handcuffs. "You know I'm not the only one in the department who works with Tom," he says moving his face to the side to speak.

"Shut up, Bridges. You're going down."

"No, he's right," I say as I break away from Luke's arms. "I overheard two other cops talking about what was going to happen to me tonight. That's why I was calling you right before this bastard hit me."

Fredrick shoves him hard against the wall. "You better give me those names, asshole."

"I'll give you the names if you cut me a deal."

"Oh, you'll tell me those names. Let's go pay a visit to our AD."

"I want my lawyer."

"Your choice, but a lawyer ain't gonna do shit for you," Fredrick says as he shoves him through the door.

"Fredrick tracked your phone. Thank God he was stupid enough not to get rid of it." Luke bends down and picks up my damaged phone.

I take the phone. "Well I needed a new phone anyway. My free upgrade is available."

When I look Luke in the eyes I can see that he's angry and upset. His face is red and his eyes wet with tears that he's trying to hold in. I fall back into his arms and let out a cry. "He was going to inject me with stuff that would put me into a coma. They did the same thing to Tom, which was how he was going to get me."

He rubs my head. "Well, he isn't going to get you now. I told you I'd keep you safe and I let you down. I should never have left you at work. I should have been there at the exact time I said and then this wouldn't have happened."

"Stop Luke. Look what came out of this. Bridges is caught and will choke up the other names and Tom is currently in a coma for who knows how long. If this didn't happen, we wouldn't have had any answers. Now all the people working with Tom will be locked up or threatened enough that they'll stop working with him."

"That's true, but it doesn't make how I'm feeling any better."

"You can't hold this much weight on your shoulders, babe. You deal with enough at work."

"It's my job to keep you safe. There are no excuses for me not to be able to."

"You can't watch me 24/7, babe."

"I can find a way."

"I want to have a normal life where you won't have to watch over me all the time or worry about my safety. I want you to be able to concentrate on your patients; they're the ones who need the help."

"Your life isn't normal and it never will be. Now the whole world knows about you and what you can do. You'll be dealing with crazy people, murderers, and cops for the rest of your life. I'll protect you and do what I can to keep you safe and that's the end of it."

"I guess you're right, but that doesn't mean I need a watch dog all the time. I'm rarely ever alone. It was also my fault. I should have stayed with Fredrick until you got there. From now on, I won't put myself in a situation where I'm alone."

"And I'll take you and pick you up from work every day. If I happen to run late then Sarah or Bobby can drop you off at the house since your mom will be there watching Michael. Is that clear?"

"Yes baby." He grabs my face gently and kisses my lips. "I love you so very much."

"I love you too, Luke."

He picks me up and carries me out to the car. "Let's get you home. Your parents and May are worried sick."

"Ugh, you told them what happened?"

"I had to tell your mom since she's watching Michael, which led to a chain."

When we pull into the driveway, my parents, May, and Charlie are all sitting on the patio furniture, waiting. When I open the car door Mom rushes over to me and pulls me into her arms. My face lands straight in her curly hair, which always smells like hairspray. But it smells good because her scent is comforting. "Honey, are you ok?"

"Yes, I'm fine. Please it's nothing to worry about." Dad overhears as he walks closer.

"Nothing to worry about?" he says raising his voice. "You were kidnapped and close to-." He shakes his head and takes me into his arms.

May walks up with Michael in her arms. I hug them both then take Michael into my arms and kiss his forehead. We all walk into the house and I take a seat on our suede couch. "You two shower and get to bed. I'll feed Michael and put him to sleep," Mom says.

"No, no you don't have to do that. It's late, and you all need to get back home."

"I insist. You need the rest more than I do." I yawn in response, on accident.

Luke puts his hand on my back to try and move me. "I'll get her to bed. Thank you all for waiting here and taking care of Michael."

"We're just glad everyone is ok and safe. I'll stay and take care of Michael for a few minutes. May, you, and Charlie are fine to head home."

May looks at me with her concerned sister face. "Are you sure you don't need me to stay either?"

"I'm positive. I love you."

"I love you too, sis." She gives me a big hug. Luke follows me up the stairs and helps me undress and get in the shower. I feel like I can fall asleep standing up. My eyes are having a hard time staying open.

"I think you need to stay home from work tomorrow."

I shake my head in disagreement, "No way. I need to stay busy. I'm not letting what happened tonight scare me. I need to work."

He puts his hands up in defense. "Ok babe." As I'm about ready to pass out my phone rings. I get up to grab it.

"Don't even think about it," Luke says. It's late, whoever it is can wait. I glance at the caller ID.

"It's Sargent Blooms. Let me see what he needs." He sighs at my response.

"Blooms, what's going on?"

"Sorry to call so late. I just wanted to let you know not to worry about finding out any more information. After the search for the woman with red hair, we had a ton of hits from random people and we found her and have her in custody."

I feel instant relief. That means I won't have to concentrate on my dreams tonight and may be able to get some proper rest. "Oh, that's wonderful news. I'm so glad you found her."

"Thank you so much for the help. I'm taking the red eye flight back to Miami tonight. I'll mail your check first thing tomorrow. Again, I appreciate this."

"Thank you and anytime. Take it easy and have a safe flight."

"Thank you, I will do. Hey, if you ever need a vacation and want a place to stay, my wife and I own a beach house we rent out to close friends and family members. I'd be more than happy to rent it out to you and your family."

"Wow, I'll gladly take you up on that offer. Once Michael gets a little older, we'll definitely be doing that."

"Great. Take it easy Linda."

"You too," I say and hang up the phone with a smile.

I look over to Luke. "Well that's one less thing I have to worry about. For once I don't anything to dream about tonight. Maybe I can sleep through without any dreams."

"I hope you do, babe." It doesn't take a few minutes for my eyes to become heavy again. I close them and soak in the darkness.

I'm standing in front of an ordinary one-story house here in Charleston. It's a beautiful day, until I hear a terrifying scream coming from the house. It sounds like a little girl and there's a weird stench coming from the house. I slowly walk up to the house trying to keep quiet and out of sight. I peek through the window and see nothing but an empty living room. I can see through the door into the kitchen. It's full of different glasses and tubes on the counter top. I see many liquids and white powders. The first thing that comes to mind is a meth house.

Shit! That little girl who was taken by her druggy father. I forgot about that case. Ok, concentrate on finding that girl. I'm surprised no one heard the scream coming from the street. I glance at my watch and the date is tomorrow. I walk around the side of the pale yellow house. I leap over a few bushes and put my hands on the ledge to raise myself up and see into the window.

The smell is definitely coming from the kitchen. I can smell it through the closed window. I look past all the glass and tubes and see a little girl, the same one Fredrick showed me, tied to a wooden high chair that's way too small for her. Her hands are tied behind, her feet are tied together with rope, and there's also tape over her mouth. She's moving uncontrollably.

A man that resembles the picture of her dad walks up to her and slaps her in the face. She stops moving and her head drops. That fucking bastard! My hand loses its grip and I fall to the ground.

I wake up as soon as I hit the ground in my dream. Luckily it's only a few minutes until my alarm goes off. I call Fredrick right away. "You need to get to this address and fast! The druggy father has the daughter in custody and is currently cooking meth and beating the child."

"Give me the address and we'll go now." I do so hoping they get there in time before the little girl is hurt worse.

After I hang up I notice I have a notification for a missed call and a voicemail. The missed call is from an unknown number. I listen to the voicemail. It's a man's very deep voice. "Don't get too comfortable because this isn't over yet." I drop the phone from my lap and stare in shock.

Chapter 19

Luke grabs the phone and listens to the voicemail. I sit there frozen, no thoughts, just fear and numbness. "This has to fucking stop now," Luke says with anger. "We're not leaving that station until this is taken care of."

Tears fall from my eyes. "Bridges did say that there are more people involved with Tom. One of them has to be the voice on this voicemail."

"I have two surgeries this morning. After that I'm leaving, coming to get you from work, and we'll go down to the station and discuss everything with Fredrick. I don't care how long it takes, we're not leaving without definite answers."

"Ok, I agree. I'm sick of this." We eat our oatmeal and drink our coffee as we wait for my mom to stop by. I feed Michael his bottle and cuddle him.

Luke kisses me as I open the car door. "Enjoy these few hours at work doing what you love. We'll take care of everything soon."

"Thank you, baby. I love you."

"I love you too." The first thing I tell Sarah is that I'll be leaving early to take care of some important business. And of course she's ok with that. She and Bobby are the reasons why my shop is still standing. They go above and beyond.

It's about 10:00am and business is still rolling. My phone is buzzing in my pocket. I place the phone to my ear and hold it with my shoulder as I make coffee. "Fredrick, tell me you got something."

"Yeah, that was the case I told you about the other day. When we walked in the ex-husband was on the ground. He died from an overdose."

I interrupt before he goes any further. "What about the daughter?"

"She's safe and alive. She's already back with her mom and the rest of the men involved with this drug case have all been arrested. Thank you."

"Of course. Luke and I are coming down to the station soon. We'd like to figure out how this can end tonight. I got a threatening voicemail from a man this morning. Even with Tom in a coma, he still has people doing his dirty work. I'm not safe yet and I'm seriously sick of this."

"Ok, we'll get it figured out. I'm working out a deal with the AD in order to get those names form Bridges. Once I have all the names I'll arrest each and every one of them. That'll take care of everything."

"Thank you, see you soon."

Luke comes in a few hours later. We eat a quick lunch that Bobby whipped up for us and head out. On the way I receive a text from Fredrick. "I've got the names and I'm going to arrest them now. It's not a good time to come to the office, but I've got everything taken care of."

"Hey babe, turn around. Fredrick just texted me." I tell him the text.

"Oh good, now everyone that was ever involved with Tom will be locked up, and Tom is pretty much dead to the water, which means you should be safe and free from Tom for good."

"Thank God, it's about time," I say with relief.

"Me too, baby. Since we're both off of work how about we celebrate a little before going home and enjoy some time together, just the two of us?"

"I think that's a great idea. What do you have in mind?"

"A nice bottle of champagne and relaxing on the beach for a while."

"Perfect." After a relaxing few hours we head home. My phone beeps again, another text.

"Everyone is arrested, and everything is over," Fredrick says. I respond to his text quickly and excitedly.

"Oh thank God!" I say and smile at Luke, "It's all over baby."

"Thank you Fredrick," he says with a smile.

***

The weekend comes around quickly. It has been nice not having to worry about Tom. I've been able to focus on my cases and coffee shop. I stop and pick up May. It's time to dress shop

149

for her wedding. Before we hit the stores we stop by my shop and I make us some coffees to go.

We walk to Modern Trousseau Charleston, a well-known dress shop. When we walk in and see all the beautiful gowns it takes our breath away. We're both speechless and our jaws drop. The lady who owns the shop comes up to us with a pearly white smile. "Would you two ladies like some help picking out the perfect wedding dress?"

May looks at her with a goofy smile. "Yes please! Your gowns are stunning and beautiful!"

"Thank you. Any one of these dresses would look beautiful on you! Did you have a type of dress in mind?"

"Yes, I'd like a strapless dress," says May.

"Alright, follow me." We spend a few hours in there trying on dresses. We don't bother going to another shop because the last one May tries on is the winner.

I look at her standing in front of the mirror in a beautiful, long, strapless dress. It's tight and fits her skinny body perfectly. The floral design covers the entire dress but it isn't overwhelming. She looks breathtaking. All three of us are in tears.

I take Michael out of his stroller and hold him facing May. "Isn't your Aunt going to be a gorgeous bride?" May smiles and tears begin to form.

"This is definitely the one."

"I agree."

"Perfect, let's get it fitted and then I'll put the request in to make the alterations." She writes down the correct measurements. "Ok, you're good to go. It should take a few weeks until it's complete. I'll call you as soon as it's in and then you can try it on again."

"I can't wait!"

We head to Bella Bridesmaids to pick out a dress for myself. May wants it to be a baby blue color. We end up finding a short but flowing baby blue dress with straps. It's perfect! We end the day at Park Café for lunch.

When I arrive back at the house Luke is cleaning the place from ceiling to floor. I smile as I see him vacuuming the carpet. "Baby, what are you doing?"

"I thought it'd be nice for you to take a break from cleaning. You just sit back and relax."

"You're sweet babe. Thank you. I'd be able to relax a little easier if you clean in your briefs only," I say with a wink.

He laughs. "Alright, your wish is my command." He slowly takes off his shirt giving me a sexy wink and then removes his shorts.

"I don't know how long I can just sit here and watch," I say as I lay Michael down for the night. Luke comes up behind me and puts his hands around my breasts and gently kisses the back of my neck and around the side of my neck. His short beard makes the sensation feel even greater. I grab the back of his neck and turn my head to reach his lips.

He turns me completely around by moving my hips. I can feel his hardness as I push closer to him. He wraps his hands around my butt and picks me up. He carries me into the bedroom and throws me on the bed. He climbs on top of me and I get up and shove him over on his back. I kiss his stomach all the way until I reach his neck, where I start sucking a little. I make my way over to his lips and kiss him hard.

He shoves me overand is inside me quickly pounding hard and fast, with my hands scratching at his back.

He raises my legs to fit over his shoulders and moves in and out slow but hard, reaching deeper than ever before. My entire body is tingling with pleasure. I tighten up, let out a big scream, and squeeze his back tensely.

We lie there naked for a little while gazing into each other's eyes and talking about nonsense. Our arms are wrapped around one another and we can't seem to remove them. Luke turns off the light and pulls the covers over us both. I give him one last soft kiss and place my head back on his chest. *Alright, let's see what this night has in store for me,* I think to myself as I slowly drift into sleep.

I'm walking down a dark alley when I spot a woman in front of me. She seems faint, almost ghost-like. I stand there with fear not sure what I'm looking at. She waves over to follow her. I follow with caution as I keep a good distance. We continue walking down what seems like an endless dark alley filled with dumpsters, gravel, and dirt.

The ghost woman stops in front of a door and puts her finger to her mouth. What the fuck is going on? She then points the same finger to the door, which magically unlocks and opens. Do I go in here or do I walk away? What if there's someone in trouble in there? If I leave what if I miss an opportunity to save someone? I sigh. "Fuck it, I might as well go in," I say out loud.

I walk up to the woman and she disappears into thin air before I can get a look at her face, but I have this weird feeling that she resembles me. She has the same curly brown hair with a thin but muscular build. The woman didn't smile once and her face was blurry. This is all too weird.

I slowly open the door but stop it when it creaks. I poke my face into what seems like an abandoned house. I walk in and shut the door behind me. I see couches and tables covered with sheets. Dust floats through the air as the moonlight reflects through the broken windows. I make my way into the kitchen, which has nothing but old, rusted, hanging pots and pans.

I stop and listen closely but I hear nothing. I walk through a dining room and see another closed door. I open it and peer down a wooden staircase. I can't see anything at the bottom because it's too dark. I find a light switch on the wall and turn it on. A light bulb flashes on but stays dim. At the bottom of the stairs there's nothing but a cement floor. I take a breath to gain the courage to walk down and see what's at the bottom.

When I get to the bottom I turn on another dim light. I look around at the cobwebs and dust. I see old boxes and a furnace. I walk around the stairs and stand still at what I see. There's a woman tied to a chair. All I can see is the back of her head. Her brown hair is damp and there's tape around her face. Her head is down and she's showing no signs of movement. My heart pounds as I walk closer to her, hoping that when I look at her face she's still alive.

I slowly walk around her and I bend down in front of her. Her eyes are closed but she's breathing. I tap her shoulder. "Are you ok?" I whisper to her. She slowly raises her head and looks me in the eyes. Her eyes are very familiar. My stomach turns and I take off the tape from her mouth. I jump back and gasp when I see the girl right in front of me. I'm staring at me.

Chapter 20

I squint my eyes and rub them to make sure what I'm really seeing in front of me is myself, sitting in the chair tied up. She's looking right back at me. She begins to open her mouth. "Linda, it's not safe. No place is safe. No one can protect you." She keeps moving her mouth but nothing is coming out. What the fuck? I begin to panic and slap my face.

"Wake up, please wake up." I shut my eyes hard and still see myself sitting in front of me. Now my mouth is moving quickly but I can't hear anything I'm saying. It's like I'm on mute. I hear the door open from upstairs.

The me tied in the chair shuts her mouth and looks up. "He's coming," she whispers. I sit back up against the wall pushing the back of my head into the wall. I hear the footsteps walking down the stairs. He's almost here. I shut my eyes, "Wake up!"

I open my eyes to my ceiling. I get up with a panic and check my surroundings, making sure I'm ok. Luke is still asleep, thank goodness, because I don't know where to begin talking about this dream. I wipe the sweat from my forehead and slowly get out of bed. I walk into the bathroom and splash cold water on my face. I glance at myself in the mirror and all I can picture is me tied to the chair.

I take deep breaths, "You're ok, Linda. That's not going to happen to you, just forget about that dream and move on," I tell myself in the mirror. For some reason I want to forget I even had the dream, erase it from my head without telling a soul.

The dream felt different than my others. It almost felt like it was fake, starting with the ghost woman. I laugh thinking none of it can be real. I splash more water on my face and then dry it with a towel. "I'm ok," I repeat to myself. I slowly climb back into bed and try to sleep again.

The rest of the night consists of me staring at the wall. When my alarm goes off I pretend to wake up as if I've been sleeping. I don't want Luke thinking something is wrong. I'm not mentioning this to anyone, not even Luke. I yawn and stretch as I turn off the alarm. We both get out of bed and continue our morning routine.

I drive myself to work because Luke is busy with surgeries all day. I go on with my day as if nothing happened. Fredrick walks in right as we open our doors. I make his usual coffee and find a seat with him. "Sorry to come in so early but we need your help."

I sit with him for about twenty minutes discussing a missing person's case. The case is about a runway teenage girl who has a tendency to take prescription meds from her ill mother. "This is off topic but I need to ask you a question," I say.

"Ok shoot," he says as he takes a sip of his coffee.

"What would it take for me to become a detective with the CPD?"

His eyebrows rise in surprise and a small smile forms. "Are you interested in this becoming your full time job?"

"Yeah, I am. I've been thinking about it and I honestly don't do much at this shop anymore except write out pay checks and occasionally serve coffee. I get so backed up with cases that I don't spend as much time here anyway. Sarah and Bobby basically run the place and I'd hand it over to them. I enjoy working with you and Arnold and the other guys at the station."

"Wow, you don't know how happy I am to hear that. I never expected this after everything that's happened."

I shrug my shoulders. "Let's just say that after everything that has happened, it has made me stronger and more confident." Images of me tied in the chair flash through my head. I ignore them and move on with the conversation.

"Well I'm glad to hear that. Let me talk with Sargent Gordan and see what we can do. He loves you and always talks about how he wishes you'd become a detective. We can probably cut out some of the requirements to get you a badge. You're already familiar with almost everything that comes with being a detective. We'll teach you how to use a gun and self-defense."

"But I don't have a criminal justice degree. Will I still qualify?"

"Absolutely. You don't need a degree with the talent you have. The only thing you'll have to do is read a book, study, and take a test. Then we'll train you as you work. That should be it but I'll double check to make sure."

"Great, thank you." He heads out the door and I get back to work. My cell phone rings and it's a New York number.

"Not another case," I say with a sigh. I answer it anyway. "Hello?"

"Hello, Mrs. Jackson?" A woman's voice speaks.

"Yes, this is her."

"Hi, this is one of the directors from the Today Show."

"As in the Today Show on NBC News?"

"Yes, that's us. We've heard many great things about your special talent. We'd like for you to fly out and do an interview with us on live television."

I feel my eyes widen in shock. "An interview on live TV. Is this real?"

The woman laughs. "Yes this is real, I promise. We'd fly you out and put you up for a night in a hotel. We'll go over how the interview process will take place, how much time you have, and review the questions that you'll be asked. And of course meet the news casters and spend some time getting to know them."

Wow, now I'll really feel like a celebrity. "Thank you so much for the offer. Can I talk it over with my husband and get back to you later this evening?"

"That's perfectly fine. Just call me back on this number. My name is Sue Strumble."

"Great, thank you Sue. I'll be in touch."

I help with the closing down process and become anxious. I can't wait to tell Luke about the Today Show and what Fredrick said about me becoming a detective. When I walk in the door I can smell something amazing coming from the kitchen.

"Mom?" I yell out.

"In the kitchen, honey." I walk into our bright yellow kitchen and see Mom standing near the stove.

"And what are you doing in here? It smells wonderful. Wait a second, let me guess. Is that your award winning meatloaf cooking in the oven?" I ask with excitement.

"Why, you're good!" I walk over and see she's sautéing vegetables.

"What's the special occasion?"

"No occasion. I just felt like making everyone my wonderful meatloaf. I know it has been a long time since you've had it."

I kiss her on the cheek. "Thank you, Mom. Is Michael sleeping?"

"Yes. He has been a joy today. Your dad is coming over for dinner as well."

"Oh great! I have some news to tell everyone. Dad walks in soon after. I give him a big hug. We sit around the table as we wait for Luke to come home. I receive a text from him saying he'll be home soon.

"So what's the news?" Mom asks anxiously.

"I'll wait until Luke gets here so I can tell everyone." We discuss what's going on with Dad's job. Flashes of me in the chair keep replaying in my head. I close my eyes and shake my head to the side.

"Are you ok?" asks Dad.

"Yeah," I lie.

Luke walks in and comes to give me a a kiss. Mom and Dad sit there and smile. Luke lets out a big sigh. "Phew, what a long day of surgeries! Something smells magnificent in here," he says as he gives my mom a hug and kiss on the cheek and shakes my dad's hand.

"I just wanted to do something special for the both of you," says Mom.

"Well that's very kind of you, thank you." We grub on some meatloaf, mashed potatoes, and sautéed veggies and we all listen to Luke as he talks about the surgeries he had today. After he's done Mom decides to bring up that I have good news.

"Linda has good news to tell us."

"Oh yeah, what is it?" Luke asks. I tell them about the phone call from the Today Show first.

"Do you want to go back on the air and talk more about your talent? It's going to draw more attention," Luke says with concern.

"I think it's a great idea. You should tell your story. You're a hero and deserve to be recognized," says Mom.

I look over at Dad. "What do you think?"

"I think it can go both ways. You'll get more attention and more phone calls than you do already, but your mom is right. You do deserve to tell your story again."

"I'll support you either way," says Luke. Yeah, he says that he'll support me but I know what he's thinking. It's dangerous. I mean there are crazy people out there who can become obsessive fans.

"I told Sue, the director, that I'd call her this evening and let her know my decision." I don't think I'll end up doing it. I just got over the Tom scandal and I don't need to be dealing with another psycho.

"And the other good news?" Luke asks.

"Well, I talked to Tom about becoming a full time detective. He said since I already work for them and I have a special talent, it won't be that hard to do. I'll need to read a book, take a test, and then they'll train me with a gun and self-defense. He's talking with Sargent Gordan today to finalize everything."

Their faces go blank with shock. "But what about your shop? It has only been open a few years and that has been your lifelong dream. Are you willing to give that up?" asks Dad with concern.

"Honestly, I love my shop and it's everything to me, but I have a special talent and I want to use it to its full capability and save as many people as I can. I enjoy working with Fredrick and his crew. I love the suspense that this job entails and I want to be able to focus fully on it. Think about how my dreams have already grown and become more stable. Imagine me putting all my focus into them and seeing them flourish even more?"

"Well, as long as it makes you happy and not stressed out," says Luke.

"The only reason why I've been more stressed lately is because of what happened with Tom. Worrying and always wondering about when he was going to attack took a lot out of me, not the job itself."

"You do have such a warm heart, so they're lucky to have you as a detective," Mom says encouragingly.

"Thank you, I appreciate everyone's support and I'm happy to make this decision. Plus I'll be bringing in more money."

"We're happy for you honey," Dad says with a smile. Luke doesn't say much. He walks around the table gathering everyone's plates. I know he's upset but it's only because he wants to keep me safe, which I understand.

I walk up to him at the sink as he rinses the plates. I put my hands on his shoulders. "I know you're not as happy and supportive as my parents are about my decision, but I've really grown to love this job. It'll make me happy to do this full time and it'll make me even happier if I get your full support."

He turns to face me. "I do support you. I only worry about your safety."

"I know you do, but I'll be working with a ton of cops, so I'll always be safe."

"Yeah, and look how working with cops has protected you in the past."

"I know, and I understand where you're coming from. Fredrick took care of everyone at the station who was with Tom, and we both know Fredrick and Arnold would do anything to protect me. They're good people and so are the other cops and detectives at the precinct. So please baby, can you be happy for me?"

He sighs and smiles. "Alright, but that doesn't mean I'm not going to story worrying about you."

"I wouldn't expect you to. I just want you to support me and realize that this makes me happy."

"I do baby," and he wraps me in his arms for a nice hug.

"Well we're going to head home," Mom calls from over the table.

"Thank you again for the wonderful dinner. Do you want to take the leftovers?" I ask.

She laughs. "Are you kidding me? You can keep them, hun."

I smile. "You're the best."

As they walk out the door, they turn to face us. "Keep us posted on everything."

"Will do. I love you guys."

"We love you too," Mom says as they turn to walk to their car.

I finish cleaning up the kitchen while Luke feeds Michael. As we lay Michael down for bed and we're about to get ready for bed ourselves, there's a pounding on our front door. "Stay here, I'll go and check who it is." Luke says as he grabs his gun.

I hear him open the door. "Come on down Linda, it's Fredrick." Fredrick? What's he doing here at this hour? *Maybe it's about the detective job*, I think, and get a rush of excitement. I bob down the stairs and the look on Fredrick's face makes my stomach turn. He's not smiling, his eyes are big, and he looks worried and angry.

My heart starts to race as I ask, "What's wrong?"

"Well we'd heard from hearsay about Tom being in a coma. I wanted to make sure that he really is."

"Yeah, and?" I ask with a trembling voice.

"I went to his jail cell today and he has vanished."

My heart drops into my stomach and my knees begin to buckle. "How the fuck can this happen?" Luke says freaking out and pacing around the living room like a maniac. "How can one fucking man have all this power? Where the fuck is he? Please tell me you know where he is?"

He shakes his head, distraught. "We can't find him. We searched the entire jail."

I stand there in shock. Maybe my dream from last night is really real? If that's the case how much longer do I have? I become light headed and sit on the couch. I put my head between my legs. I don't even shed a tear, I'm so in shock.

Luke is still pacing and he becomes so angry that he punches the door. "Fuck it, I'm going to look for him." He begins to open the door, while I still sit there in fear. The sounds around me seem to echo.

"No Luke stop, don't be stupid. Look at Linda right now. She needs you by her side at all times. Leave the searching for Tom up to my department."

"Then fucking start searching for him!" he screams. The echoes start to fade and I lie down.

"I already have my men out looking for him." Luke continues to mumble curse words as he walks around.

Fredrick walks over to me and kneels beside me. "Linda, don't worry we'll find him."

"That's what you keep saying, yet he keeps getting away," I say bluntly with no emotion.

"I know, but I mean it this time. I won't stop until I put a bullet through his head."

I nod in agreement and continue to stare at the white floral designed ceiling. Fredrick gets up and walks over to Luke to try and calm him down, "Luke, relax and take care of Linda. Let us handle this."

"Obviously letting you handle it hasn't been working very well."

"I promise man to man that I'll end his life."

"If you don't I will, and I mean it. I'm not scared to kill that son of a bitch."

"I know you're not, but you won't have too. Keep an eye on Linda. I know this is very far-fetched, but it'd be best if she stays awake for as long as she can. It's too dangerous for her to sleep."

"That shouldn't be hard," I say as I get up off the couch. "I'll drink tons of coffee." I walk over to them. "I didn't want to mention this to anyone, but I had a dream last night. I saw myself trapped. I didn't see the man who trapped me, but it has to be Tom. I saw myself and talked to myself. That has never happened before. I know he's close and the next time I fall asleep might be the last time."

Luke's eyes widen and he looks over at Fredrick. "She can't stay awake for too long, so you better fucking find him."

"I'm on it," he says walking out of the door.

Luke takes me in his arms. "I'll stay awake with you until this is over."

I look him in the eyes. "Luke, what if it's never over? Tom is determined and smart."

"Don't say that. I'm not losing you again."

I hug him and realize that my time is almost up and I know it. I've come to the realization that this is the end. There's no way they can find Tom in time. I won't be able to stay awake for more than a day.

I walk upstairs and hold my baby boy. I don't know how much time I have with him so I want to cherish every moment, because soon enough I know I'll be waking up in that chair tied by my hands and feet with no one to save me.

Chapter 21

"Linda, you have to try and keep your eyes open," Luke says as he shakes me gently.

"I'm trying but my eyes are so heavy." I'm struggling beyond words right now. My eyes feel like they weigh one hundred pounds. My vision goes in and out as my eyes open and close.

"Here, take another sip of coffee," Luke says as he hands me the cup. I take a small sip but it's not doing anything to help.

"Baby, I-I can't stay awake." My eyes slowly start to shut and they stay shut. I can vaguely hear Luke in the background.

"Linda, fight it." But his voice fades and darkness takes control.

I slowly open my eyes. I feel pain shooting through my entire body. I moan as I try to move my head. I see flashing dim light as I fully open my eyes. I try to move and realize that I'm restrained by something. I see a brick wall in front of me. The lighting is dim.

I look down and notice that I'm tied to a chair. I know exactly where I am and that there's no getting out. I open my mouth to scream for help and I taste blood in my mouth.

"Oh God, please find the strength to help me. I don't want to die or worse still, be in the presence of Tom for the rest of my life." Tears fall as I try to move more. My body is sore as if I've been beaten. I sigh and stop moving.

I hear footsteps coming down. Oh shit. My heart pounds and my stomach growls with hunger. As he approaches I feel more panicky. I hear him turn the corner. "Why, she's finally awake." I hear the deep raspy voice that belongs to Tom.

He turns the entire chair around so I'm right in his face. "Well aren't you glowing today. You've been taking a good beating these last few days. Don't you remember anything?"

"Why are you doing this?"

161

"Oh silly naïve, Linda, don't you know the answer to that already? I told you that I'd get you and have you all to myself. I told you that you'd be mine. I keep my promises."

"How did you do it?"

"I can't give up my secrets or else that would ruin this fairytale ending."

"Ending? You do realize that Fredrick and the entire police department are searching for you, let alone my loving husband who wants to kill you?"

"Ha," he laughs loudly. "They'll never find me. I made sure of that."

"I wouldn't be too confident."

"Well let's get this party started," he says as he unties the rope to my hands and feet. Fuck, what's going to happen? Don't show fear. Don't let him win.

He picks me up and carries me up the stairs. I have no energy and I'm too sore to fight back. *"First I need to feed you before we start to play. I don't want your energy to run low."* Play? What does he mean by play?

He shoves rice and bread down my throat and gives me sips of water. I never thought those two foods would taste this good. I'm starving. *"What are you going to do with me?"*

"Oh honey, what I've been dreaming of for so long." Chills run down my back and as he speaks to me, my body won't stop shaking. Stop it Linda! Show no fear! Maybe if I stay confident the whole time, he'll give up.

"Alright, now that you've been fed it's time to begin." He carries me up the stairs and into a bedroom. I try to fight him off by holding onto the sides of the door. He shoves my arms down and throws me on the rough, springy bed.

"You're not getting out of this one, my pretty girl." He ties my hands and feet to the bed post. *"I want you to truly be mine,"* he says licking my cheek.

I move my head side to the side and spit in his face. *"You'll never fully get me. I won't allow you to have that power over me."*

"Oh, I will have that power over you, just you wait and see. You're going to be begging for more by the time this is over. You won't even remember that bastard of a husband of yours. He took you away from me, and now I'm taking you back."

He walks over to a dresser and pulls out a pair of scissors. He cuts *my shirt right off my skin and throws it onto the ground. Then he cuts my bra and throws that aside, too. He looks me up and down and licks his lips. "Wow, you're more beautiful than I ever imagined. I can't wait to get a taste of that."*

I get angry. "You, piece of shit, won't get anything from me. You won't get my satisfaction and you won't get my pain. You don't deserve any of it!"

"Hmm, I like confident Linda, it makes me want you even more." He then cuts off my shorts and panties. He stands up and undresses himself looking at me with an eerie smile. "I finally get what I want, and what I'm about to do to you is something you've never experienced before. You'll cry out wanting more, you'll forget about Luke and every other man you've ever slept with. I'll be your last lover forever."

"Fuck you."

"Oh, you're about to baby."

He climbs on top of me and I glare into his eyes. "You know, the sad thing is you're too weak to actually have me in person. You have to pussy out and capture me in a dream. This isn't even real life. So what you're about to do is fake. How does that make you feel? Are you too scared to come to me in person? You're afraid Luke will beat your ass into the ground like he did once before. You're too weak of a man to do the real thing."

His eyes widen and his face reddens. He slaps me across the face. "You fucking bitch."

"Awe, poor Tom can't even get a hard on? What is this anyway? Luke never has a problem with that. He can always pleasure me beyond anything I could ever want. But you, you're just a lousy lay." He slaps me over and over. "What? You want me passed out so you can concentrate better? That makes you even less of a man. You can't even fuck a girl while she's alive and awake." He becomes furious, cursing every second. Then he jumps off of me and paces around the room talking to himself.

Wow, he really is fucking crazy. He's speaking to himself as if there's someone standing right in front of him. "Yeah, keep talking to yourself and see where that's going to get you. You're a tiny, weak man."

"You better shut the fuck up or I'll end you right now."

"Go ahead and kill me. I'd rather be dead than be with a limp and useless man such as yourself." I can't believe I'm talking like this. I have no idea where this strength is coming from, but I nourish it.

It's obviously working, so keep going!

"She's just using you," he talks with himself. "Don't listen to her; she's trying to get to you. Be a man and do it!" he yells at himself in the mirror. He takes a deep breath and turns towards me while breathing heavy and grunting. He opens a drawer and pulls out a knife.

"Are you ready to be mine forever, Linda?" he says, pointing the knife at me.

I smile at him. "Bring it." He slowly walks forward and then BAM! A shot to the head sprays blood on the walls and his limp body falls to the ground.

I cry out in relief. How the fuck am I getting out of here? I look around trying to find an escape. I feel as if someone is pounding on my chest. What's happening? Please someone save me. My vision fades. And darkness takes over.

***

I slowly open my eyes. The bright light shining through makes it tough. I move my head slowly as I try to figure out where I am. That's when I hear, "Mommy?"

I'm taken back by surprise when I hear someone call me that. Why would anyone call me that? "Shh, let her fully wake up." I hear a familiar voice. Is that Luke?

I lift my head. "Luke?" I call out.

"Yes honey, I'm right here." I see his warming smile in front of me and I begin to smile.

"Mommy?" I hear again and I look at Luke with confusion.

"Don't be scared Linda, someone wants to meet you." I begin to tear up when I realize what's going on.

I look beside me and see a handsome young boy of about six years old. He has beautiful bright blue eyes and resembles Luke. "Mommy, are you ok now?"

Tears fall from my eyes. "Michael?" I say with shock.

…To be continued

About the Author

Megan Johnson began her writing career in 2013. She has had a passion for writing since she was a little girl. She is from Charleston, West Virginia where she works as an Elementary School Teacher. *Dreams Become a Nightmare* is the sequel to her first novel, *Dreams Become Reality*.

Her writing career began with poems, which were published in the *AB Influx* magazine through her college, Alderson-Broaddus University.

Megan plans to continue writing books. Be ready for a thrilling end to this Dream Trilogy as she prepares her third novel. To read more about Megan and her writing career please visit her website, meganjohnsonauthor.com.

Other Books
By Megan Johnson:

Dreams Become Reality
(part 1 of the Dream Triology)

CPSIA information can be obtained at www.ICGtesting.com
Printed in the USA
BVOW06s1459161115

427318BV00014B/31/P